W9-BNO-173

BEAUTIFUL DREAMER

BEAUTIFUL DREAMER

A Novel

Christopher Bigsby

THOMAS DUNNE BOOKS

ST. MARTIN'S PRESS

NEW YORK

THOMAS DUNNE BOOKS.
An imprint of St. Martin's Press.

www.thomasdunnebooks.com
www.stmartins.com

Designed by Bryony Newhouse

Library of Congress Cataloging-in-Publication Data

Bigsby, C. W. E.
    Beautiful dreamer : a novel / Christopher Bigsby.
        p. cm.
    ISBN-13: 978-0-312-35583-8
    ISBN-10: 0-312-35583-1
    1. Men, White—Fiction. 2. African American boys—Fiction.
3. Male friendship—Fiction. 4. Racism—Fiction. 5. Hate crimes—
Fiction. 6. Tennessee—History—20th century—Fiction. I. Title.

PR6052.I35 B43 2006
823'.914—dc22

                                                                    2005046745

First published in Great Britain by Methuen

First U.S. Edition: August 2006

10 9 8 7 6 5 4 3 2 1

To my wife Pam, with much love

BEAUTIFUL DREAMER

He was awake. A moment before and he had been running in his dream, knowing it for a dream but helpless to allow that knowledge to still his terror. Now, though, he was awake, tense, ready for flight, but staring up at the ceiling, not knowing it for what it was, at first, not knowing where he was until he calmed enough and knew for sure what he should have known right away. The room was dark, moon and starlight pinched out by the clouds of a summer storm. His dream had been lit by lightning, pulled into the dream to make the invisible visible, but now there was no more than a smother of darkness and an unfamiliar smell. It was burning flesh, he told himself, feeling the sharp pain. And yet that was not the smell. It was something other, something musty, familiar yet out of place. It was a human smell, dank, sharp-edged.

Then he heard the soft slide of wood on wood and a dull punctuation to that slide, a window closing, eased down and closed. Had they followed him here, then, come to finish the business they had begun with clubs and a whip and a tyre brace heated in the fire until it was white at the heart and red at the tip, sparks flying off it like a Fourth of July sparkler? They were interrupted then, though not before they had started to spell out their message on his chest, him screaming so that he could hear nothing else, except that he did, he had, as the metal burnt a letter, a letter whose shape he could not tell even though it was being inscribed in flame on his own skin. He heard the sizzle like meat in a skillet, and smelt the smell of that meat. Yet he was detached, even in his agony, trying to fix that smell when you would think there was no space for such thoughts. Until then, pain had been a word like any other. This was pain like he had never known it, so that the word 'pain' flew away, language flew away in the scream that seemed as strange to him as to those who looked on, eyes gone soft and crazy, jaws slack. This was some mystery they were witnessing. Well, to hell with them, he thought now, though, not then. Then there was no space for such thoughts.

If it hadn't been for the lights, twin beams slashing through the trees, not lightning though, that had flickered and flashed like in a stage play, like the only stage play he had ever seen, *Uncle Tom's Cabin*, with the girl escaping over the ice floes, if it hadn't been for the lights, like shining daggers from the eyes of a devil, who knows how it would have ended, if it was ended, as the slithering slide of a window closing suggested it was not. Would they have stopped at spelling out what they wanted to say, turning him into a writing slate, a school lesson for all those foolish enough to do what he had done? Or would they have used the rope that one of them got out of the trunk of the Dodge along with the wheel brace, as though trying to make up his mind which way to go, except what other direction could they have had but hell?

They were people he knew. Not people he liked or had much to do with, having as little to do with people as he could, people being the source of trouble. But they would give him the time of day and he would nod to them and say 'Fine day', or 'How much is them beans?' But they were not people he knew any more. Something had gotten into them and changed the way they looked and talked. It was like they had been hoodooed or whatever it is that happens when your soul is taken out of your body and replaced with something else. They weren't neighbours any more, nor people either.

And how they got that way was beyond him and needless to know. They were freaks of nature, he said to himself, though not to himself because he heard the words spoken in the darkness and, though the voice sounded strange from the rope they had tightened round his neck before they decided on fire, he knew it for his though he had not meant to speak aloud, what with his knowing that someone was there or had been there, depending on whether he heard them coming in or going out, that sliding sound of wood on wood.

He reached for the gun he had propped by the bed, leaning on the orange crate where he put his fob watch each night, the one left him by his father and to his father by his father. It had taken him some effort to fetch it from the kitchen when all he wanted was to lie down and sleep and maybe die, but not at the hands of those who had chased and then treed him at last when the lightning stilled everything like a photographer's snap. So he had found it, resting where it should be, and opened a box of shells, the cardboard damp from the air but the shells clean and sharp and smelling like they should. And he had loaded both barrels, though his hands were burnt where he had tried to push the brace away, burnt and cracked so that one at least was already a claw, wouldn't do what it should, especially since it was shaking, since he was shaking and feeling so sick and faint that he knew he could pass out any time now. But the need to load it, to slide and click those shells into the smooth, oiled metal, kept him going until they were in and he was staggering, like a drunk, to his bed and leaning the gun against the crate before falling into a dream in which he was chased again through the same woods, knowing, again, that it was a dream, but knowing, too, that he could never get away, as you know such things in dreams and still manage to behave as if it isn't true. At the same time, part of his mind knew that he was lying beside a loaded shotgun and that if things got bad and they began to close in again, all he would have to do was reach across and there would be his gun, its red-orange shells lying ready so that he could end the hunt, and the pain, in an instant, though when he put it there, he meant it only for those who might have followed him across the river and along the track to this cabin, or if not them, then their dogs, dogs that could seek you out in the middle of a storm and his soul in the middle of hell.

~

When he woke again, a flat grey light entered through a small window, one part of which was replaced by cardboard, fringed around with white where the rain had forced its way in. The walls, papered with newspapers and magazines, peeling here and there like leprous skin, were a patchwork of dull colour. Whatever he may have been dreaming disappeared the moment he opened his eyes. The pain of his chest drove out everything else and he let out a cry. 'Shit!' Outside there was an answering call from a bird, which echoed through the woods. He glanced across at his shotgun. It was where he had left it. He reached for his watch, but there was nothing there. It was always there. It was how his day began. Then he recalled it all, recalled why there was no watch, why the gun was there, why his chest was afire, why the hand he held in front of his eyes was black-red with blood and seared white on the palm. He remembered, too, the sound of the window, unsure whether he had dreamed it or not, for already dream and reality had begun to braid. For the moment, though, the most pressing need was his aching bladder. A burnt chest and a burnt hand took second place to the need for a piss. He smiled at the irony, surprised he could smile at all. He sat up. 'Shit.' Sitting up was not so easy. There was a scuttling beneath the bed. Scuttling sounds meant nothing. They were like the bird calls, more noticeable by their absence than their presence.

To reach the outhouse, he had to go through the kitchen, moving slowly and carrying the shotgun under his arm. The Negro boy sat at the table, a small bundle wrapped in a piece of red cloth clasped in both hands as though it were that which held him in place. He sat so still that the man did not see him at first. He was focused on moving with as little pain as possible. Then he did see him, and stopped, the two staring at each other. He had been ready for just about anything, but not for this. This was what had got him close to being dead and now here it was again. Maybe it was Death come to tap him on the shoulder. What did he care for black people? He hadn't cared for that other one and it had got him a rope round his neck and white iron on his chest from those who didn't listen, wouldn't listen, didn't want to hear in case it spoiled their fun. And now here was another of them, sitting in his house as if he had a perfect right, as if he had been invited, as if he didn't care that he brought death with him. On the other hand, he knew that if he didn't get to that outhouse soon, he would wet himself, and that suddenly seemed to matter. He couldn't do that in front of a nigger, even if to those who wanted him dead he belonged with them rather than his own. So he shifted the shotgun some but went right on by the boy as if he weren't there at all and out back where the outhouse, door half-open, was set just free of the trees and far enough from the cabin so that the smell wouldn't reach and the flies would stay where the shit was. He only just made it in time, fiddling, with his torn and burnt fingers, to free himself and even then getting some of the hot liquid over those fingers and into the cuts. And when he had finished at last, and the soft patter from below had ceased, he still felt he wanted to go some more, but after a moment or so the feeling eased. He didn't button up. There was no urgency now that would make him risk his fingers again. He wondered whether he needed something else but the shock or whatever had ended any need of that for a while.

He felt faint, having pissed, and almost sank on one knee, but, remembering where he was, stopped himself and instead lifted the door to open it again. The air was fresh from the storm and the sun had already begun to burn the water off. Wisps of steam lifted from the warm wood. He looked around. There was no sign of anyone. No doubt they were all still drunk. There had been plenty of jugs and bottles the night before, glinting in the flames of the fire. How had they lit a fire in that storm? They must have come prepared. Gasoline. Rags. Dry wood. And the rope if they couldn't get it hot enough. That left the nigger. What was he doing in the kitchen? What was he doing in the house at all? Got to get him out or the whole thing would start over again. Not that it would make any difference. Like a dog downing its first lamb, once they got a taste for it there would be no stopping them.

He walked along the path, slick from the rain. There were no other footprints than his own, and his smeared from where he had dragged himself rather than walked. So the boy had come the other way. He kicked the back door open, so as not to risk his hands. The boy sat where he had left him. He could have been dead except that his eyes were wide open and those eyes followed him as if he were the curiosity and not the other way about.

'Well, boy, who the hell are you and what for you're in my house?'

The boy said nothing, but stared back at him. Dumb insolence, he thought, who had heard the phrase before when he spent two summers at school before his mother took him out to work the fields. He had heard it again, too. 'They's either downright insulting, speaking straight to your face. Or they don't say a damn thing. Dumb insolence, that's what that is.' Harley had said that down in the store. He served niggers because they had money, not much but some. They had to go around back and they had to pay what he charged, but he served them and there were those who said he shouldn't. Then one chose the front door and look what that had brought.

'Boy, I'm talking to you. What you doing here?'

And that was all he did say because a great wall of darkness rose up from the ground and swallowed him so that he knew he was falling but couldn't do a damn thing about it except worry what would happen when his gun hit the ground. But he didn't worry about that for long.

This time, when he woke, he was on the kitchen floor, but instead of lying crumpled where he had fallen, he had a blanket over him and the boy was holding out a cup of water, as if he had every right to be there in his house, in a white man's house. But he hadn't had a drink for more than a day, not since the rainwater dribbled through his lips as he ran through the waving trees, slimed with green. He took the cup, but his hand was shaking so that he spilled it, a snail smear on the blanket. The boy took the cup back and dipped it in the pail, holding it out again. He reached for it but the boy shook his head and pulled it back. Then he held it out again. This time he raised himself on one elbow and let the boy put the cup to his lips. He swallowed that cup and two more besides before lying back and staring at the ceiling where a fly paper, black and crusted, curled up on itself.

How could he have got into this? What was the man to him? And who was this nigger boy?

Then he was asleep again and did not wake until the afternoon sun slanted down through the yellowed window. The boy sat where he had before. He looked up at the window. The burnt flesh had begun to tighten and the pain was suddenly more than he could bear. His hand was curled tight and when he tried to open it a knife seemed to slice through him. He knew he couldn't lie there and yet movement seemed impossible. The sunlight fell across his face and he drew on the energy it seemed to offer, gritting his teeth, grinding them together so hard that the ache began to balance the pain that flowed through him. The boy began to get up but then relaxed back into the seat, watching this burnt man try to rise from the flame of his agony, watching him as he rolled on his side like a dog, as he pressed down with his one good hand, the hand they had twisted behind his back and thus protected from the fire, and raised himself like a wounded bear. He watched as he knelt, one hand down, the other balled, his face twisted, eyes shut, and then, breathing deeply, raised himself up, towering over the boy but swaying like a tree cut through and ready to fall. He staggered without looking, eyes shut against that sun which none the less gave him hope to think he could make it, carry on, staggered to his bedroom and collapsed on his bed, head hitting the wall, orange box toppled.

It was some time later, how much he could not tell since his watch had been taken from him by those who were not so far gone as to forget to steal anything worthwhile even though they told themselves they were driven by something else, when he came to again. He could see it was later because the sun was slanting down on the coloured picture of a movie star half-peeled from the wall as if she wanted to climb in there with him.

He remembered then what he had forgotten. He had forgotten his gun which was in the kitchen with the nigger boy, the nigger boy who had entered his house like a thief but taken it into his mind to stay. And who could he be but Johnson's boy, assuming Johnson to have had a boy, as how should he know who knew nothing of him until he was stupid enough to step in front of him when he should have let things lie, take the course they had always taken and always would? Who else of his kind would have sought him out? So here he was, to make sure that this time they would kill him for sure, who would have done before but for the lights coming through the woods and, since hardly none of them had automobiles, who could that be but authority? And you never knew about authority that has to watch its back and maybe do things it wouldn't do if there weren't those around to see. But how could he get rid of the kid when he couldn't take more than a step without collapsing?

Then all thoughts sank somewhere too deep for him to hold on to them as a wave of pain rolled over him, spun him round so that his back arched up. Then it was over and he was lying limp and sweating, even though the heat of the day had passed, was passing. And when at last he opened his eyes the boy was beside him, looking down without an expression in his eyes beyond interest, as you might look at a squirming snake run over by a truck, twisting itself inside out as if it could survive a broken spine. But then he saw that the boy had something in his hands. It was a jug. He hugged it to him instead of hooking his finger through the arched neck, as any man would have done, but it was a jug just the same and it was the one thing, he knew, that might help him through.

They had beaten him a while with a fence post while the fire heated up and he had heard a couple of his ribs crack as you would snap a twig for kindling, but he knew that nothing vital had been damaged. He wasn't dying, just broken here and there and marked so that he and others would never forget, would remember what they wanted people to remember. What he needed was to get through the next few hours, next days, so that his body could mend itself, because weren't no doctor would come on out and where was the money to pay him if he did? The jug was two-thirds full and the boy had sense enough, whatever else was on his mind, to know that whiskey could do what a doctor couldn't or wouldn't.

He beckoned him forwards with his good hand and when he stepped close reached out and took hold, letting the bed take the weight for a second and smelling that smell he had smelt before, not unpleasant, just different.

'The cork, boy,' he said, nodding his head, unsure whether he could ease it out himself. The boy just stood and watched and did nothing.

'What they call you?'

The boy stared back at him, dumb as before. After a moment, though, he turned around and went back through into the kitchen. So, no name.

He removed the cork without trouble and, curling his finger through the handle, lifted up the jug, using the back of his hand as a lever. His lips were bruised and swollen where he had been punched, cut where a ring had caught him, loosening a tooth. The whiskey stung, but it warmed him right away, flowed through him. He choked, spilling it on to his neck, and that gave him a thought. He rested the jug on the bed to get back his strength and then lifted it again, pouring it over his chest. He cried out and smelt his burnt flesh along with the whiskey, but poured a little more before setting the jug back on the bed again. He rocked with the pain, mumbling a jumble of words that meant nothing to the young boy who stood in the doorway and watched as, after a time, this deranged white man began to sing 'Amazing Grace', every now and then dropping in an obscenity or raising the jug to his mouth to drink in the oblivion that was the only cure he knew.

When he woke, he knew that he had passed through something and out the other side. The sun was streaming in again, but it was another day because it lit up that part of the wall that meant morning, lit up another set of pictures, mostly of women but pictures of countryside, too, and the interiors of houses he would never see, gleaming white and clean and full of cookers and Frigidaires. His chest felt cool and he saw that a piece of cloth had been laid on it. And there was the boy still, ringing out another piece, not realizing he was awake and watching him. Why hadn't he just robbed him and run off while he could? Not that he had anything worth robbing, except his gun. And he was worried about the gun. The boy shook out the cloth and looked up. Their eyes met. For a second, neither moved. Then the man said, 'That's real good. Put it on, son, but be careful how you do it.'

For a second or so, the boy stood, unmoving, and then he leaned forwards and gently lifted off the piece that had been lying on his blackened chest, dropping it into the bowl before putting the new piece on. It was cool and soothing and at last his head seemed clear. He knew he was through the worst, that he would be better, provided they didn't come looking for him, as he was afraid they must, having been interrupted in what they were doing, having been frustrated so.

'What's your name, boy?'

The boy looked at him for a second and then shook his head.

'Cat got your tongue?'

He nodded.

So, the cat had got his tongue. What was he supposed to make of that? He was maybe dumb? Anyway, what did it matter? He wasn't in need of conversation and wasn't anyone else going to come and see him, not one person he knew who would care to admit acquaintance, still less make their way out to his shack and lay cool cloth on him, as the boy did again now, lifting off the old and putting on the new as if he understood the cool it brought. And each time a smell renewed itself, the burnt flesh, the young boy, the whiskey, almost washed away now by the cloths but not quite gone.

'You get me the gun,' he said, jerking his head in the direction of the kitchen as if the boy didn't know well enough where it was. The boy stood watching him. 'In the kitchen. You reckon you can carry it? Don't play with it none. Just bring it through to me.'

Still he stood there as if trying to make up his mind whether to obey, or maybe not understanding, since he had no idea how bright this boy might be who didn't seem bright enough to be able to talk. He seemed to make up his mind and stepped through into a golden shaft of light so that it looked for a second as if this little black, insignificant thing were made of the purest metal. Then he was gone and the man listened, still not knowing who this boy was and whether he wanted him dead. Besides, all he had to do was walk away and why he hadn't he couldn't figure, any more than he could why he had done what he had and why everything had happened as it had, though at the time it had seemed as inevitable as the sun rising in the east. Maybe the boy would walk back in and lift the two blue-black barrels to his head and blow him past everything and into perdition. He could feel his pulse pick up and start to speed, like a mule sensing home.

The boy carried the gun with both hands. He gripped it

around the barrels and carried it upright, stock just above the floor, as though it were something in church, something holy.

'Hand it on here.'

The boy did as he was told. It was as he had left it, the shells still in place. All he had to do was pull the twin triggers and he could blow his troubles away, or more likely anyone who chose to come and finish what they figured, maybe, they had only just started. He leaned it against the wall where he could reach it, watching the boy as the boy watched him.

'We got any food?' he asked, aware that he had put the two of them in the same sentence by using the 'we' as if the boy had a perfect right to be where he was, sliding in through a window without being asked and dumber than the day he was born unless he were truly born that dumb.

'Food. We got any?'

The boy shook his head. So he had been looking for it, when he himself was beyond all thoughts of food or anything else. Even so, it seemed to the man that he must be right because he had been meaning to take a turn about and get him a rabbit when it happened, that and what he had meant to buy at the store and hadn't in the end because of what happened. What he had really bought was a pitcher or two of trouble that poured right on out in the dust when that nigger started everything going, because, when it came down to it, it was that man, black as night, walking right on in the front door, who had started it. So there was no food and him hungry suddenly, who had thought such a short time before that he would never need food again, that the world consisted of pain and little else besides.

'You find something,' he said. 'Berries. Something. You know where you can find something to eat?'

The eyes stared back at him and he could see this boy wasn't going to go anywhere unless he scared him or talked him into it, and he sensed that scaring him wouldn't do it since he could just head on out and leave him on his own.

'I'm OK now,' he said, as if the boy might feel an obligation, though why he should surely beat him, beat him all ends up, unless he were Johnson's pup, and, just thinking it, he could see how it must be true. But even if he were, why should he think this a place to come, a white man's house where he knew, if he wasn't dumb in his mind as well as his voice, that nothing good ever come from the white man as long as white and black had sweated together under a Tennessee sun which didn't give a shit what colour you was, no more than the mosquitoes and flies and bugs, which bit and burrowed and fretted their way in pulsing clouds. 'I'm OK now. I'll be all right. Just find us some food or we'll starve. And where's the whiskey?' The boy looked down and the man followed where his eyes were looking. The jug was on its side, empty as could be, and the only others he had were buried or hidden and he wasn't about to tell him where, not yet at least, not until he had let the string out a mite further to see how far he would run. Then the boy was gone, so silently he never noticed it. Maybe he got Indian in him, he thought, Comanche or Pawnee or some such, though the Indians he had seen were a sorry sight, sorrier than him and he knew how bad he must look, how bad he had looked since his wife had died, his wife and his son, one hour apart, the pain of one caught up in the pain of the other, neither one saying anything at the last, or making a noise, neither one making a sound except her long last sigh as though she needed to breathe out all twenty-two years of her life in a single breath before she could move on, giving that life back to the wind that stirred in the trees without cooling the air. Well, that was long ago and a lot of nothing had filled the air since then.

On a sudden thought he broke the gun open and slid the shells out. Why leave a loaded gun where the boy could maybe pick it up and shoot him where he lay? He had not done it when he could but who was to know? And if it were Johnson's boy, then what had happened to his father? Well, he didn't have to be told to know what that might be, to know what it was. They weren't going to leave it at that. When they were hitting him with the fence post and pushing the tyre brace in his face, saying they were going to take his eyes out so he couldn't no more look at a woman than that nigger would ever be looking at another, he knew what they had done to him, to that black man who walked through the door, as should have known better, and talked back and touched a white woman. He knew what they had done but he didn't know it all. Was it just stringing up or was it something more? They were still hot with it when they caught up with him, so that he knew it must have been bad. Then they told him some things, and how was he to know if they were true, how was he to care, who had troubles of his own enough?

And now the boy. Had he seen it happen or had he just come upon it when it was all done? And why was he here, who should have been running already, running as fast as he could go, knowing even at his age, whatever age that was, that they would be after him and that they would never stop until they got him unless they just run out of will, decided they would rather torture a cat or poke the eyes out of a dog or do things to their sisters or mothers or whatever it was that had made them spawn, the way they did, people who were no more people than the mule he'd owned before that took sick and he couldn't earn a dollar for hauling wood no more or hire her out to the farmers. Question on question rolled into his head until the weight of them was more than he could take and he swam into a darkness that took him into it as if it were a memory wrapped in a dream and buried in the warm earth. So he was asleep again, which was the only way he could mend, though being asleep he could no more tell himself that than he could know that he was a man lying in a bed and waiting for someone to come and tell him it was time to die.

That night, he lay in that bed, tangled and matted with blood still, and watched the shadows trembling on the walls. The lamp hissed steadily and outside was a blanket of sound: rasping, croaking, sudden cries like someone screaming far away. He had to think. The pain was still there, but steady now, steady so that you knew it would fade in time. What wouldn't fade was those in town, those scattered in cabins hidden in the woods. He had to calculate whether they would leave him be. And if they wouldn't, well, what then? He had kin of a sort a hundred miles north but they never had truck with him or he with them. Still, they were family and if need be, well, they could give him a bed until he got himself work. But this was his place. It had been his father's place, too. Neither one of them had made anything of themselves, his father coughing through the night and finally giving up on it all and being taken into town to be buried. He remembered his mother, but not as anything much more than a shadow floating above him. He had a picture once, though heaven knows how they had been able to afford it as couldn't afford shoes or much else besides, including food. He had kept it a while but it had got lost and he didn't look at it so often that he noticed. Well, it was gone now and so were they, and all he had got was this cabin and an outhouse and neighbours who maybe wanted him dead. And how was he to get work now, after this? Cutting trees, working in the field, fixing fences, all depended on someone stopping by and asking him to come on over. No one was going to stop on by now.

Then there was the boy standing there with a rabbit in his hand, holding it up as a cat will lay a mouse before your feet to show what she can do. There was a piece of line around its neck, though it didn't look like a snare. Its head flopped down and he could see where it had been hit with a rock. So, the boy had got talent, knew what moved in the woods and how to make it move in his direction.

'You done good. Skin and cook it. There's maybe some potatoes and a carrot in a box by the door.'

Maybe there were. To tell the truth, he couldn't remember. Living on his own, he bought when he had need and not otherwise and had no memory of whether there was anything to put along with the rabbit to make a stew, assuming the boy could skin as well as catch and cook as well as skin. One thing was sure, for the moment at least it was the boy would have to do everything. Come tomorrow or the next day and he could fend for himself, but come tomorrow or the next day and there might be more to worry about than finding potatoes and carrots and cooking with a rabbit or anything else. He glanced once more at his gun, still within reach, still with the power to resolve all his problems in one way or another.

The boy was in the kitchen. He had done well with the rabbit, except that there was nothing but a single carrot and a sweet potato and no salt, so it had been pretty thin eating. Even so, he would never have got by without him. And him a nigger, the thing they had named him for with their tyre brace heated in the fire.

'You. Come on in,' he cried.

A chair scraped in the other room and in he came, carrying a stub of candle that he blew out since the lamp lit the place well enough, bringing a cloud of bugs and moths banging against the screen which was rusted in places so that some of them got through and fluttered up and down the lamp, sending shadows dancing over the newsprint, making the images in the magazines appear to move and stand out.

'Sit yourself down.'

The boy sat.

'Not there. Bring it round where I can see you. If you can't talk, I want to know if you're telling the truth. You know what the truth is, boy?'

The boy looked straight back at him, then slowly got up and dragged the chair round closer to the bed. He sat on it and it rocked a little where the joints were giving out.

The man eased himself on to his elbow.

'You Johnson's boy?'

At first, the boy simply stared back, the light glistening on his eyes. Then he nodded his head.

'You know what happened got me here like this?'

The boy shook his head.

'Foolishness,' the man said, and lay back on the pillow, tired again, suddenly drained of the strength he had thought was coming back, the strength that seemed to flow through him with the rabbit stew.

'It were at the store,' he said, though as much to himself as to the black boy sitting in this white man's house. 'I were in for some nails. I were looking in the barrel and sorting them out and in he comes, in comes your father, not going round back like he must have known, like he did know, he should have done. He comes in and lets the screen door bang closed. She had been in back, Miss Emily, who I'd known at school all them summers ago and who was no good then, though she was only eight or some. She come in drying her hands with a cloth and looking across to me. I don't think she even saw him at first, not expecting to and so not noticing him standing there. I didn't say nothing. It weren't my job to say nothing. They made the rules, they could see they was kept to. Then she saw him all right and dropped the cloth she was so surprised. "What the hell you doing here?" she said, in a voice could crack eggs. "I've come for some seed, I thank you, mam."

'I swear she started to move toward the seeds before she realized what she was doing. Then she shouted out again, calling to her husband. "Harley, come in here. There's a nigger come in the front." Then she picked up a rake. Could have been anything, but that just came first to hand. She picked it up and she walked toward him as if she were going to sweep him out of the store, as if it were no more than a brush, though the tines on that thing could take your eyes out.

'I don't know that she knew what she was doing, but she pushed it in his face so he had to put his hand up and when she kept on pushing he twisted it out of her hands. Perhaps it was just the shock of it that made her fall, or perhaps she was leaning forward so that taking it away left her nothing else to do but tumble down. You listening?'

The boy sat as he had before, except he leaned forward a little, focused on the man in the bed, his chest cut up, his hand drawn together.

'Anyway, just then in he comes and sees this nigger standing over his wife, the rake in his hands. "Rape," she said, as if she didn't know what it meant, as if she thought it was what you said when any black man, any man, perhaps, lifted a hand against you. You understand what rape is, boy? You sure better because that's what they'll get you for just like they got your daddy.

'"No," I said. "Your wife made a swing at him. She just fell when he took it off her." I don't know why I said it. It were no business of mine and, besides, what was he doing there when he should have been round back, knew he should have been round back?

'"Rape," she cries again. Then he gets smart, except too late, I guess. He turns around and opens the door, letting it go behind him and was down the road before her husband comes out with the gun. "It were an accident," I says to him, and he swung around and I thought for a moment he was going to let me have it right there, right in the chest. "Nigger lover," he said, and I could see his finger tightening on the trigger. Then he swung back and was out the door, but he was too late. Your daddy had got away. Only not for long, I guess, not for long.'

He reached out for the cup of water on the orange crate and swallowed it down. Then he lay back and looked up at the ceiling again. Something slithered across it and down the wall so fast you couldn't see what it was.

'You there when it happened?'

He looked at the boy. His eyes were full of tears. They rolled down his black cheeks, glinting in the light of the lamp as though molten metal were flowing over pitch.

'I guess you was. They told me some about it, you can be sure. They told me about it before they got to work on me. Not everything, though, as I guess. You don't have no mother, do you?'

The boy shook his head slowly, but he wasn't looking at the man any more. He was staring into space, staring at a wall full of words and pictures. He was somewhere else.

'Took him out back, so they said, and shot both his legs out from under him, then strung him up. Strung him up, then let him down, then strung him up again. That's what they told me. All for going in the front door and not letting a woman, a woman with no more brains than a skunk, not letting a woman jab his eyes out. I lived here all my life and kept myself to myself. I don't have nothing against niggers. They keep their-selves to theirselves, too. My daddy thought they was no better than animals, but that was because his daddy could remember when they was slaves. Not for us. We never had that kind of money. But being slaves made people think they was animals. They got their lives, is all I think. I can't say as I would care to live alongside them, but there's lots of folk I wouldn't choose to live beside.'

And so he might have gone on, since talking proved to him that he was alive and recovering, and talking to himself was the only company he had had. But then he heard a sound he had never heard before, a wail that cut deeper than the white-hot wheel brace. It was the boy. He wasn't crying. He had simply opened his mouth and this sound had come from somewhere deep inside him to fill the room. The man made to say some-thing but then could think of nothing to say. He relaxed back in the bed. Who would have thought niggers would take things so bad, he thought, and remembered what he tried hard not to remember, the death of his wife and what it did to him looking down at her as if it were impossible she could have gone away, impossible that what lay in the bed was no longer her but just a place where she had stayed a while.

After a time, the boy stopped the noise and they both listened to crickets and frogs and invisible creatures beyond the screen living their lives as though there were no such things as men and women who lived and died and were kind or cruel. After a while, he eased himself up on his elbow again.

'Boy, I had nothing against your father and I got nothing against him now, even though he brought me this trouble. I know who's at fault here and it weren't him, except that he should have known better than to go through the front door.' He stopped, unsure why he was saying what he was saying.

Then he continued. 'Give me the box down in the corner over yonder. Pass it over to me.'

The boy followed his gaze to a shoebox with a fine silt of dust on it. He got up slowly, as if all the strength had left him, and bent down to the box. He could see how nobody had looked at it for a long time. There were loops of spider's web attaching it to the wall. He picked it up, brushing the web with his hand, and took it across to the man before sitting again. The man swept his good hand over the top, clearing away the dust, and then opened it carefully. He looked at it as if deciding what to do and then slowly took the contents out one by one, laying them on the soiled sheet. He looked at them again for a time and then picked up a small glass jar and eased the top off.

'Cream,' he said. 'For the hands.' He plunged two fingers into the off-white mixture and sniffed at it. The boy could smell the perfume. It reminded him of a flower, though he couldn't remember which. The man smelt it, too, and he wasn't smelling it to see if it was still good. He was smelling the past, so that for a moment it wasn't the past any more. Then he smoothed it gently on his other hand, the hand that was still closed and tightening. It seemed to ease him somewhat because he lifted the cloth from his chest and began to smooth it over the letter burnt into his chest, the letter which was black but which now shone yellow-white in the lamplight. The letter 'N'. The boy looked at it.

'You know what that stand for?' asked the man. 'That stand for you. That stand for "Nigger". Only there was supposed to be another letter. An "L". It was supposed to spell out "Nigger Lover", only they never got to finish it. Not that time, at least, because someone come along and they weren't so brave that they were willing to stay around and be seen for who they were. What you think of that? You like that written on you?'

Then he paused as a thought came to him.

'I don't suppose you need it. You already got it written on you and you can no more get it off than I can. But they no different. I guess they don't need nothing written on them for folks to know what they are. You just look at them and you know.'

He went back to putting the cream on and then eased the top back on the jar, twisting it so it would fit back again. The room smelt of flowers. He had seen his wife put the cream on to soften her hands and he figured that if it could do that for her, it could maybe soften the harsh brittleness of his scabs.

'You best be going.'

The boy looked at him, an old man, no doubt, as it seemed to him, face scraped as though they had pulled him along the road, scabs forming down his cheeks and on his nose.

'Get back to your kin.'

The boy did not move. They stared at one another as if they could hope to understand each other, one black, one white, one young, one who would never see fifty again, never see anything again since it was past and gone and there was little he cared to recall.

'You can't stay here. How can you stay here? Look around. Nothing here for you.' Then remembering there was doubtless nothing elsewhere either, his father strung up in front of him and him lucky not to follow. What stopped them? They didn't usually stop, just went on killing until it was all out of them, whatever it was took them over, and wouldn't be satisfied until there were bodies swinging like Spanish moss from the trees. He shrugged. Time enough tomorrow.

'Find yourself somewhere out back. You're not sleeping in here.'

The boy got up now, glancing back at the man in the bed as

if to confirm what he had said. Then he was gone, though what he would find was beyond him since all there was was the kitchen or maybe outside on the porch where anyone passing might see him. But who would pass by here, unless those others came back? And if they did, it would be to finish their work anyway and a black boy lying on the porch would make no difference.

The lamp was losing power but he didn't have the strength to pump it, could feel sleep waiting anyway. For the moment, though, he looked down at the sheet, streaked red and black, and saw the shoebox still there and around it the things he had taken out in looking for the cream.

There was a small brooch, with a purple stone. She had worn it once, the day they married. It was all she had been given by her mother who had tried to stop her marrying, 'throwing her life away' as she said. There was no particular shape to the brooch, not a flower or an animal. He held it up to the fading light. It had a glow at its heart. The gold metal had begun to flake but, as he turned it, it seemed to him that he did remember something from that time, not the day, not the night even, just a feeling he hadn't known since, had forgotten he had ever had. He put it down and looked to see what else he had swept into the box the day she died, when he wanted to get rid of everything that reminded him not of her, not that, but of all that had happened. For as long as he could recall, he had had nothing. Then he had had something, something that seemed more than he could ever have hoped for. Then suddenly there was nothing again, only this time a hundred times worse. The baby was nothing. It had meant something to her and therefore to him, but the loss of the child was supportable. Everyone lost a child or two, or, if not that, then whatever they were carrying when hard work, or hunger, or desperation made it or her give up on it. This one was born, even if it did no more than open its eyes and decide against it. But it meant worse than nothing for in opening its eyes it closed hers and he was back in the dark again, each day offering nothing but something to be got through.

There was a book. That was hers, too. He couldn't read more than a few words and neither could she, really, except that this was a gospel. He could make out the name: John. He never saw her read it, but she held it sometimes, would sit out front in the dappled shade and smile as if she knew something he didn't. And lastly there was a piece of cloth, blue, a piece of cloth she had kept for the child and never got to use. And that was her life, all contained in a shoebox that had never held shoes, at least not for him, since he had picked it up from the rear of the store where it had been thrown by those who didn't realize that everything had its use.

He put the things back in the box, everything except the cream, which he put on top of the orange box. And when it was all in, he pressed the lid back on and reached down and slid it under the bed where he could reach it if he should need it, though why he should need it he didn't know. He looked across then at the only other thing that had come into his life with her: a piano. They had argued about it, but it cost them nothing, coming from her home when her mother died at last, bitter to the end. She could pick out a tune with two fingers so you could recognize it most of the time. She could play half a dozen hymns and 'Beautiful Dreamer'. Two of the notes didn't play, more, now, for all he knew, and it sounded tinny from not being tuned. He had thought to throw it out, set fire to it outside and listen to the wires stretch and break, but he had no more been able to do that than he had been able to throw out the shoebox. He couldn't play himself, never even ran his fingers along the yellowed keys, though he would brush the dust off the lid from time to time just to see the shine. He glanced across at it now, hearing, as it seemed to him, as he had not heard for so many years, the sound of a tune picked out by two fingers at day's end. Then he turned the knurled wheel on the lamp and the dark swallowed him, the hiss of the lamp stilled so that those other noises could fill the room. He lay back, feeling already that the pain was not as great, that healing had begun. There was a time when he would have said the Lord's Prayer. He didn't do that any more, not since she died and he had put her life in a shoebox. Instead he formed her name with his lips but didn't speak it aloud, was unaware, even, that he did so, and within a minute slipped off to sleep with the smell of another time filling the room.

For all that he had slept so much, he was sleeping again now as if his body knew better than him that rest was the medicine he needed. And since he could afford no other, it was just as well. So he floated down and since his wife was on his mind as the heaviness descended on him, it was of her that he dreamed. He was meeting her again at the dance. He remembered the smell of pine planks from the barn, so new you could see the curled roses of wood where they had been shaved by the plane, lying around as if someone had just got married and these were the cast-offs from the bouquet. She looked all angles, arms and legs sticking out from her cotton dress, but there was something else besides. She had a smile on her, not the blank face of the others, and you could see the way her body shifted under the dress as if she'd as soon tear it off and run through the grass under the moon as go dancing in a barn that smelt of fresh pine. Then he was walking with her as though the time in between had gone, walking with her and looking up at the trees. She had wanted to leave, wanted him to come with her.

Talked of Birmingham one way and New Orleans the other, and he knew it was all a dream but he liked to hear her talk, knowing that neither of them was going anywhere but where folks had always gone.

She was young, always young, and young again now as the sun edged up across his blackened chest and touched his lips and moved on, night having turned to day, flowing orange-yellow over his crooked nose. She smiled, and he forgot all that followed, since it hadn't happened yet, forgot the sickness, the coming time, the tearing that left her more like a rag doll than a person, and though he was sleeping and the years had taken the pain and turned it into something else, or so he thought, even so, tears trailed down his ruined face and started him into wakefulness again at the very moment the sun laid a golden bar across his eyes. Doubtless it was that that woke him, and when he opened his eyes he had to close them again right away and assumed it was the glare that had made his eyes water and not feelings he thought he had buried along with her body where the pines rose up from the sandy soil and seeded themselves, where he gave her to them that seemed to need her strength and beauty to lend to their own.

They came as he knew they would, as he had assumed they must. He was stepping out of the outhouse when he saw them on the other side of the clearing, one with a rifle under his arm, the other with one trailing down. They saw him the moment he saw them. It was the Steadman brothers, or two of them, the twins, faces seemingly squashed, known for their meanness, not caring who you were if you were in their way. His first thought was for his shotgun, left behind in the bedroom. It might as well have been in a different county.

They stood still at first, looking around, making sure they

were alone and that nobody was going to interfere. They stood and watched him as if he were no more than an animal they had surprised, as if they might be on their way once their curiosity was satisfied. Except that he knew they were here for a purpose. There were no dogs. Guns but no dogs. They were hunting, all right, but not anything that needed dogs to run them to ground. Then they started across the clearing. If he had not been broken and in pain, he might have made a run for the house, which was no more than forty feet away, but, the way he was, he had no hope of reaching it. Besides, they had maybe only come to gloat, there being no one to watch what they did, to urge them on, give them the courage they didn't have. They preferred the odds in their favour, as they had been before. Neither was the one had held him when the iron was put to his chest, but their brothers had done it and their faces weren't so different, after all. They had been there, faces lit by the fire, long, broken faces, as if something had pushed them out of shape. They swung around to put themselves between him and the house, knowing, no doubt, what was in his mind. Everything seemed to stand out with sudden clarity. It was as if a photographer had brought the scene suddenly into focus so that it seemed unreal in its precision. The two men stood out like characters on a stage. Everything else seemed to fade away.

'Morning,' said one of them, he didn't know which, having never been able to tell them apart and not caring for the most part, either.

He nodded.

'Got banged up a deal?'

He stood his ground, mind racing but getting nowhere.

'Seen any squirrel?'

'No,' he said, knowing they weren't hunting, except for him.

'They're about somewhere.'

'So?'

There was a pause. The boys looked about again, checking they were alone.

'How're things ... nigger lover?'

They had come right round now so that they stood between him and the door. They had moved around slowly as if out on a stroll. The one with the rifle over his shoulder brought it down, slowly, casually, as if he might not know what he was doing. The other spat brown liquid into the dust and wiped his mouth with the back of his sleeve where a strand of saliva was hanging down.

'That's what you are, ain't it? Nigger lover.'

'You boys want something?' He knew what they wanted and couldn't see how they wouldn't get it.

They looked at each other as if sharing a joke. 'Hear some nigger got hisself strung up. You hear that? One of your relatives?'

They were building the rhythm so that what would follow would seem natural when it came. They shifted nervously, awkwardly, like young boys at their first dance, half serious, half not.

'Got some nigger woman of your own, I s'pose. Got her in there, maybe.'

He jerked his head toward the house where the boy was, where the boy would stay if he had any sense, though who knew whether he did or not. Coming here hadn't suggested such, but who was he to talk who had got himself into this by not minding his own business as he should?

A soft patter of rain began to fall, making the leaves nod and dance. The men showed no sign of noticing. They stood side by side, their bodies looking dislocated, the rain picking at the ground around them.

'We got some business, you and us. Never finished what we was doing the other night. Wouldn't you say? That right, ain't it?'

'I don't want no trouble.'

'Oh, hear that? He don't want no trouble. Is that right? Why, then, we just be going, won't we? Got a knife, brother? Seems now might be a good time to finish.'

He looked at his brother and smiled, not moving, looking back now at the man who could feel his legs begin to shake, begin to go, a weakness flow through him as though his body were getting ready to surrender.

'Seems we ain't. Going. Seems we stopping some. How you like that? Them apples? Seems we ain't going, after all. Stay around some. Have us some fun. What you say?'

One of the two, face lop-sided, a grin fixed on it since birth, reached behind him, his hand reappearing with a Bowie.

'Got a sharpening stone? Seems to me this's a mite dull on the edges. Point's all right, though. Nothing wrong with that.'

They took a step toward him. He took an involuntary step back.

'Hey, hold on there. Ain't time for you to be going. We got us some business.'

'Yes,' said the other. 'I got a question for you, nigger lover. Which is it to be, the knife or the gun?'

And suddenly he found himself welcoming the question, welcoming the chance to end it all right there. What lay ahead for him? Here was a way to put a stop to it. But not like this, not from them.

They were no more than twenty feet away from him now, slightly to the side as if inviting him to make a run for it, though there was no possibility of that.

'Hell, Mikey, I think he wants the gun.'

At that, they both swung their rifles up, not lazy now but meaning business, side by side like gunmen in some western.

'You looking at the end. Just should've known better, wouldn't you say? Man gets to be as old as you. Think you'd get a parcel of sense. You ain't got no sense, though. Went against a white man, a woman, too, white woman. Don't matter she dried up and stupid. She white. One'n us.'

They both eased the weapons in their hands, looking around like hawks, searching for movement in the trees, looking everywhere but where they should. Then they tensed.

'Got any prayers, nigger lover? No? Guess not. Well then, go to hell.'

The shot was a surprise, though he had been waiting for it, bracing himself, his mind a whirl of images he couldn't hold they went through his brain so fast. It seemed to explode from nowhere. But instead of him falling, one of the brothers seemed to rush forward as though to embrace him and then fell just a few yards short. The rain came down as if the shot had opened the gates of a dam. The other brother, unbelieving, took half a step forward, looking down at his own gun as if he had done it himself, and then, realizing, swung around just in time to take the second barrel full in the chest and stagger back, turning as he did so, so that the man could see his chest a mess of black and red, with a wisp of smoke.

And that was it, or almost it. The black boy stood still, the rain coming down like knives around him, the gun still pointed straight ahead, though there was nothing in it now, both barrels being fired. Then the rain stopped, as if someone had given an order, but still they stood as if neither of them could think what to do next. There was a groan and the first brother moved an arm like something that had been run over on the road.

The man walked past him and stood in front of the boy who

hadn't moved since that last shot had been fired. He took hold of the gun, easing the boy's fingers from the trigger. Neither spoke. He looked back for a second at the two men lying in the mud, one dead, as it seemed, the other, perhaps, not. Then he went inside. He went across to where the shells were stored in their cardboard box and took one out. He smoothed the water away from his eyes where it was dripping down from his hair and, flipping the two empty cases with finger and thumb, slid the shell into one of the chambers. Then he closed the gun, clicked it back into shape and swung around to face the open door. He looked at the kitchen, as if bidding it farewell, and then strode outside where the sun had suddenly lit everything golden bright. He walked past the dead brother, seeing he was dead from the way he lay and not needing to check on him. He stood over the other one, face down, hand moving. There was a strange noise coming from him, nothing you would have called human if you had been asked to identify it, but a noise that showed he wasn't dead. He hooked a foot underneath him and flipped him over. There was a groan.

His mouth was open so you could see he had no teeth worth mentioning, more gaps than teeth and those he had were pointing every which way but where they should. His eyes were half-open and there was a smile on his face, the smile he had been born with. The man looked at him for a moment, as if making up his mind about something, though the fact that he had gone inside for the shell showed that he had already made his mind up about what mattered most. Then, as if recalling where he was and what he was about, he stepped back half a dozen paces, brought the gun up and squeezed the trigger. The body leaped up and then settled back. He broke the gun open straight away, letting blue smoke drift up in the sunlight. The birds had stopped singing for a second, but now they started up again, not caring who lived and died or what the purpose of it all might be.

He turned around and walked back to the cabin, gathering the boy up under his arm as he walked past, unaware, it seemed, that this was the first time he had ever touched a Negro, let alone held him to him as if he were kin.

He sat the boy down and went out again, returning a few minutes later with a jug under his arm. He took a broken cup from the sink and poured the shine into the cup, placing it in front of the boy, who was shaking as if some engine were idling inside of him.

'Drink it.'

The boy shook his head, tears welling up into his eyes.

'Drink it, boy. There weren't nothing else to be done. First it would have been me and then it would have been you. You did what you knew you had to do and that's all there is to it. Now we got to bury them boys and get out of here or we'll both be as dead as them two wanted to make us. There's more of them Steadmans and won't nothing stop them coming for us, if they know they was headed this way. Our hope is they was on their own, thought this whole thing up theirselves. Either way, we got to go and I need you all together.'

He lifted the jug and tilted it into his own mouth, swallowing hungrily. He realized that the pain had left him, that he couldn't feel the burnt chest or the burnt hand. He nodded to the cup and the boy slowly lifted it to his lips, his hand shaking.

'Drink it up, boy. You saved us both but that won't be worth spit if we ain't away from here within the hour. Goddamn it, why can't you speak?'

The boy lowered the cup, a trail of liquid down his chin glinting in the sunlight from the open door. Then he raised the cup again and drank, his Adam's apple bouncing up and down as he drew the heat into his cold body.

*

He knew they would have to leave. He thought to bury the bodies, even carried a long-handled spade outside with the idea of dragging them into the wood and digging a grave, two graves in the black soil. But when he stood over them, the handle of the spade already paining him when he tried to grasp it, he knew that he could never manage it. Even dragging them the thirty or forty feet was probably beyond him and certainly, if he did manage that, he could do no more than scrape the surface away. The dogs would find them straight away. The boy was useless, still sitting inside and sobbing. And how old was he anyhow? Twelve maybe? Fourteen? He couldn't tell with them, had never been able to tell, nor cared over much, not needing to.

He thought of the well. If he could get the boy to lift the legs, they could maybe drop them down where they wouldn't be found, not for a while at least. But he doubted he could manage it, and besides, the idea of them rotting down there, poisoning his water, even if it wouldn't be his water any more once he had gone, wherever he was going, for the truth was he was vague about that, was more than he could face. And what did that leave but letting them lie where they fell, shot through with hatred, brought down by their own evil. Nor was he sure what the law could do, whether, if he put enough distance between this place and where he would end up, that would mean he was free and clear, he who had never been free and clear of anything.

Then there was the boy. It came to him then, as it had not before, that the two of them were tied together. He had seen the boy shoot the men and the boy had seen him finish that one off. Besides, the boy had saved his life, even if it was him, or his daddy, who had put that life at risk. Either way, there was no place one could go without the other. So he was tied to a dumb black boy who would have looked through him as he would have done in turn if they had met on the street.

He went back inside, knowing now that they must be on their way, that even now there might be others making tracks to the cabin. It stood to reason they would have told their brothers, unless they had been off on their own and just took it into their heads to have some more fun. Even so, it was a matter of time, especially since he couldn't bury them as he should, since he had left them where they fell. Then there was the law to chase them down.

He looked around the place that had been home and wasn't any more. He felt nothing about it. He tried to figure what he should keep, what he should carry away with him to wherever he was going, but could think of nothing. In the end, he opened the cardboard box and took out the jewel, glinting deep in the sunlight, not knowing why he did it, and tore a piece of paper from the wall. He wrapped it and thrust it down into his pocket. He took his clasp knife and he took the seven dollars he had hidden beneath the floorboard under his bed, where the cockroaches scuttled each night and the dust was thick. He went into the kitchen and opened the box of shells, filling the pockets of the torn green jacket he slipped on, the jacket that would make him sweat in the day but that would be needed at night.

He filled two dishes with the cold rabbit soup and put them on the table.

'Eat.'

The boy shook his head.

'Eat. We got a long way to go and no time to stop to find something.'

Again the boy shook his head, so he went ahead and ate his own bowlful, listening as he did so for dogs or shouts or anything that would tell him he was too late and should have gone already.

'Look, boy, you and me are together. I dare say you don't like it, and neither do I, but if you stay, you are as dead as those out there, the one you shot and the one I shot. They won't ask you nothing if they catch you and they won't shoot you clean as you done. You seen what they can do and there's more they can do when pressed to it. So stop your crying and eat. We going in couple minutes.'

The boy looked at him as if trying to understand what he had been told. Then he reached out a hand, still shaking, his face still streaked with snot, and slid the bowl towards himself. He took up the spoon and ate the stew as if he weren't human, as if he were a robot doing what the machinery said he should do.

Five minutes later, they left the clearing. The sun was clear of the trees and the shadows had shrunk back so that the two dead men lay in a circle of light. The man led, heading for the stream, knowing that they had to kill the scent, but knowing, too, that that would be what those who followed would expect. The boy had nothing on his feet, while he had his old boots, holes everywhere and with newspaper lining the sole. The water was ice cold from where it came down from the hills. It ran fast but was only deep enough to cover their ankles. At the edge, you could see where they had stepped, but the water would soon smooth that out. The man glanced back to see that the boy was following, knowing that he would be since he had no choice and that the stream gave them a direction when that was what both of them needed above all.

The woods were alive with noise and the sunlight flashed on the water and sparkled where it filtered down through the leaves. His body was feeling better. He had hardly felt any pain sincc he had stepped from the outhouse and seen the men standing there with their guns, deciding whether to kill him or not, or simply when.

Further down, as he knew, the stream would join up with the river and then whoever followed would have to decide which way they had gone. It would be harder to walk in the river. It was deeper and faster, but they would have to stay with it as long as they could because the men would simply run their dogs up and down the banks until they found where they had come out.

The boy had stopped crying and was looking at the water, trying to pick his way among the rocks. He moved easily enough. The man didn't feel anything about the killing, though he had never killed a man before and wouldn't have now if he had had a choice. But he wondered how it was for the boy to do what he had done. He did it for himself, no doubt, figuring that if they killed him, he would be next. Even so, he had picked up the gun and stepped right into the light and where would a nigger have had a chance to fire a gun before? And instead of firing both barrels, as he had done when his own daddy had let him heft it for the first time, the boy had squeezed only one, swivelling round to take the other man. And that man was looking him straight in the eye and pointing a gun of his own. No, this might be a boy, but he was a boy with something inside. And was he born with the dumbness, or had the dumbness come with what he had seen? There were stranger things.

They walked for an hour and then the woods opened up as the stream rushed towards the river.

'You swim?' asked the man.

The boy nodded.

'Best way is to pick us a piece of wood and go with the current. Keep ahead of them.'

They would expect him to go downstream, figuring, as had he, that it would take less energy and be faster, too. But the trade was the speed.

There were logs aplenty fringing the river, nudged there by the eddies that swirled along its edge. He made sure that they both had one. For a few hundred yards they waded, but outcrops of rocks soon forced them into the twisted water, flecked white, so that they both let the river carry them, lifted their feet and drifted as fast as they could have walked in the open. The cold was pleasant enough, numbing his pain, washing away the memory of the guns in the clearing and two men lying dead for eternity.

He lost a sense of time, watching out for rocks, being spun around, dragged forwards, sucked down. He lost a sense of distance, there being no way to judge such with the trees swimming by in a blue sky broken into fragments, with the sun sparkling through branches and shining bright off still water where a sandbar left a stretch satin-soft beside the ruffled fold of the moving river. He had lost all sense of feeling down below, lost all sense of feeling almost everywhere except in his face, with the spray smarting and blinding him. He was pulled onwards, where the river decided the direction and the speed, not knowing where it was going except away, swallowing water, coming up for air, looking where the boy might be but seeing nothing, spun again.

He stopped not because he chose to do so but because a patch of land reached out into the river and a branch snagged him and swung him in to where his feet touched the black mud, not that he felt anything but the fact that it was there. And then the boy smashing into him so that he almost lost his grasp. They hung there for a while, gathering themselves, before he edged along toward a place where he could ease himself out of the water. He didn't look at the boy, assuming that he could look after himself, not caring either, just reaching for the land, cold through and done for.

The first few steps, his feet sank into the soil, but then they got a purchase and he forced himself forwards but soon fell to his knees and then over on to his back. And though the sun shone down clear and hot, he still felt cold through, as though the ice at his centre would never melt. He was aware that the boy was beside him but it was the cold that dominated. He began to shake, though he was out of the icy water now and in the sun. It was as if the sun had triggered it, as if only now did his body realize how cold it must have been.

So they lay, side by side, forgetful, or so it seemed, of the reason for them running, the reason for lending their lives to the river in the trust of getting them back. They lay, tired through and cold, while the sun slowly worked to bring them back to life.

At last he sat up and saw that the gun was still in his hand. When he first jumped in, he had held it above his head, but after a bit had forgotten it was there at all. He looked at it in surprise, trying to figure out how he had held on to it all that time when he couldn't feel anything and had had to put his hand out to steady himself time and again. It was there, though, and he had to use his other hand to pry it free. Then he realized something else, something he should have thought about if there had been time to think of anything at all. The shells were in his pockets and his pockets had been under water. He reached in and took them out one by one, his fingers still cold, still difficult to use. There were eight shells and though the cases looked waxed, so that beads of water stood out on them like trembling diamonds, he was not so sure they were any good.

He lined them up side by side on the dark soil, orange-red, like so many bright eggs put there by some creature no more than a moment before. His own clothes were steaming and he figured the same sun that was warming him at last might dry out the shells for when he would have to use them. For with the sun and the warming of his body had come remembrance of why he was running, why they were running. He began to think of the boy who was sitting a few paces off, breaking a twig between his black fingers and staring into the passing river, thinking thoughts of his own, thoughts perhaps of the father he had lost and where they were going.

'You OK?'

The boy looked around, as if unsure where the sound might have come from. Then he looked across and nodded.

'We wait here a bit and dry out, then we move on. There's a railroad somewhere up ahead a piece. I thought maybe we could get ourselves a ride, get out of the county.'

The boy showed no signs of being interested, no sign that he would rather be on his way.

They had been going some hours, he knew that. He had lost a sense of the time of day, except you could always tell within an hour or so by watching the shadows. The sun might seem pinned in place and immovable, but if you watched the shadows you knew it was edging across the sky. He flexed his fingers, the feeling now fully returned. But there was no pain in his chest, though he seemed to remember you were supposed to keep burns dry. No chance of that, and the plunge into the river had done him no harm that he could tell. There was a bruised feeling from his ribs but the burn itself seemed to have settled down.

'Let's get going.'

He picked up the shells, one by one, warm now to the touch,

and dry, and dropped them into his pockets, four in each. He broke open the shotgun and squinted up at the sky through the barrels, light spiralling down and two circles of perfect blue at their end. Water wouldn't have done any harm, not so long as he got to clean it out sometime soon, a little oil, a piece of cloth.

He got to his feet and looked around. There was a path of sorts, which was not what he had wanted to see. That meant that people came this way and it meant that anyone following wouldn't be slowed. But it would be foolish not to take it. The thing was to reach the railroad and hope there was a freight passing sometime soon. There were those that came this way on boats, but he had never done such himself so he knew nothing about this stretch of the river beyond the fact that it took him where he wanted to go. If he had travelled by land, he would have taken another direction, circling around. They had come a fair way, though how far he did not know. And the path had not been there whenever he had glanced across, trying to keep himself floating, trying not to run his head up against rocks, so anyone following would have had some trouble unless they took to the water themselves and that didn't seem likely.

He struck out along the path, the gun over his shoulder and the boy walking behind. Who would have thought he would have found himself doing this and with no one but a black boy for company? Well, you did what you did and took what came when it came. There was no other way to live he had ever found.

~

I see him coming. He's coming fast. The cart is swaying side to side and I can see where he using the whip, which is something he never do. Something's happened, right enough. I'd finished peeling the potatoes and weeding out back and was just sitting there before having another crack. Then he comes. He pulls back on the reins and is off before she's stopped.

'Get you things together. We going.'

I don't know what he means. I can see something has happened but I don't know what and none of it makes any sense.

He stopped and looked down at me, trying to decide, perhaps, whether to explain it all. And he does. He squats down there in the dust and takes hold of my arm.

'I done something stupid. I went in the front door of the store.'

That didn't seem too bad to me. I know we get to go in the back but using the front door don't seem to me such a crime.

'More than that, I got to having a tussle with them all. Might have been shot dead right there, hadn't of been for a white man.'

'A white man.'

'First time I ever know anyone stand up for one of ours. Jake Benchley, over past Richmond's place. Anyhow, I got out of there but I put my money on they coming after me. We got to get.'

He looked at me a moment more and then was off inside. 'Get some clothes and put them in a bag. Then get some food and the bottles out yonder.'

'Yessir,' I said, not knowing even then what this was all about. I guess we took about an hour loading things up on the cart. I got some water for the mule, which looked pretty dead from being ridden so hard. It only took us an hour but it were an hour too long. We weren't even up on the cart when we spotted them. Rain had been coming. You could see from the sky. But it hadn't come yet so the dust still rose up when anyone rode along and there was dust rising up now. My daddy squinted his eyes to see who it was. Then he knew.

'You got to get out of here.'

'I'm staying.'

With that, he hit me with the back of his hand. He never done that before but he did it now and it hurt.

'You going.'

'Where?'

'You get to your aunt over Hastings. You know how to get there.'

'Yessir,' I said, none too sure that I did.

'Well, then, get going.' Then, in spite of what he had said, he reached out a hand and pulled me to him. He lifted me up in the air, big though I was, and gave me a kiss, right on my lips.

'I love you, son,' he said, and hugged me to him so it drove out all the air. 'Now get going and don't stop for nothing, you hear. Things work out, I'll come get you.'

Things didn't work out, not at all. I ran off into the bushes. I could see them now. The dust was still round them but there was half a dozen or more, on horses. They were riding hard and I could see they rifles. I turned to run but couldn't. Instead, I lay down there in the deep shade among some bushes. Nobody would see me there but I could see everything. I could see more than I wanted. A whole lot more. Even though I couldn't believe it, I saw it all.

They were down off their horses before they even stopped, leaving them to wander off, trailing their reins. My daddy just stood there on the porch and watched them come. They stopped a way off, as if they didn't know what they had come to do. I couldn't hear what they said, but one of them was shouting and my daddy was answering back. For a minute or so, they just stood like that and then one looked to where I was hiding so that I thought they had found me out, but of a sudden they rushed toward him. He hit one so that he fell straight down, and another, who swung away holding his face. But then they were on him and started in to beat him. I could see how they were fighting to have their turn, pulling their fists back and hitting him hard as they could. It were terrible to watch but not as terrible as what they did next.

One of them went across to his horse and unhitched a rope he had over his saddle. He walked back, paying it out in his hands. Then he started to fashion a loop at the end and I knew what they were going to do. I got up, meaning to rush out and put a stop to it, but I remembered what he said and I knew that they wouldn't pay attention to me, so I lowered myself down again, feeling so weak in the knees I thought I would fall.

They dragged him across the yard to the barn and threw the rope up over the beam where the pulley lifts the grain up. Then they fixed the rope around his neck and straight away lifted him up. They all hauled on the rope and I could see how daddy's neck twisted to one side. Then one of them let go of the rope and took hold of his legs and pulled down on them as hard as he could. Then they all stepped back, still holding the rope. And I screamed, except that when I did nothing came out, nothing at all. I screamed but it was all quiet except where they were hollering. Then they tied the rope off and stepped back, as if to admire what they had done.

They went inside the house and I could hear where they were trashing it. Then they came out and turned around to watch as a drift of smoke came out. Then pretty soon I could see flames at the windows and then it was licking out of the door and around the doorposts. Then there was a kind of whoosh and the whole thing seemed to lift up in a mess of flames. I could feel the heat from where I were lying.

Their horses started getting skittish so they got back up into the saddle and headed out. But just before they got clear, one of them turned his horse, reached back behind him and brought a rifle out. Then he steadied his horse, took aim, and fired a shot. I see where it hit my daddy in the chest and sent him swaying. But I don't think he felt it at all. I think he had gone when they first pulled him up.

Then they were off and I ran out. I ran straight to him where he was swaying still. I tried to undo the rope but it were pretty tight. At last I managed it and it slipped right through my hands. He fell to the ground and I ran up to him, the heat from the fire making me put my hand up against my face. The rope was tight. I tried to get it loose but couldn't, it was so tight. There was a knife inside but the house was nothing but a mess of flames now. He was bleeding from where the bullet had hit him but I knew that he was dead. I still tried to get the rope undone and at last I eased it off him. He just lay there, settling a bit. His face had been squeezed up tight when the rope was around him, but now that had gone his face smoothed out. I tried to cry but wouldn't nothing come. Not a sound come out of me though I was heaving so I was sure I would be sick.

After a bit, the heaving stopped and I gave my daddy a kiss. I knew he was dead. I knew they had killed him for going in the wrong door of the store and I knew I had to be going. What could I do but what he told me, only I was afraid that they would know where my aunt lived as well, that they wouldn't be content with killing him. I sat for a while and watched as the roof of the house collapsed in a swirl of sparks and then, some time on, the walls fell in. The heat was burning me but that didn't mean much. What did that matter? I thought to bury him but the tools were inside, except for one that wasn't. I had been working the garden and the spade was still there. So I spent the next several hours digging a grave. The soil was loose and it wasn't so hard but I got the length wrong at first and when I tried to put him in he was all doubled up. But after a while I managed it and then sifted the earth back on top of him until it was done. I was sweating from the heat of the day and the fire, though that had burnt down to a red glow by now. The earth formed a little mound and I stuck the spade where a cross should go. Then I said 'When I lay me down to sleep' and stood there a bit, crying. The tears came down but still there weren't no sound. It was as if my voice had got swallowed up by all that had happened.

I knew, now, where I was going. I wasn't going to no aunt, at least not yet awhile, until I knew what they were all up to. But I was going to seek out the man who had tried to stand between my father and those that wanted to kill him. Maybe he could save me and explain what it was all about. He was white and maybe he could stop them doing what they might have a mind to do next. I didn't know no white man but perhaps he had the power to do that. So I ran off through the woods and kept running until I snagged my foot and fell so that all the wind went out of me. Then I just sat there and couldn't go on. Everything that happened seemed piled on top of me and I couldn't move. I had seen what they had done and it seemed as if the world was done with, too. I started in to cry but no sound came out. I just cried and hugged myself because there weren't nobody else was going to no more. And I was scared as I had ever been. And I had got turned around and wasn't sure for a while where I was but I guess that was just because things had happened.

Then it started, like I'd known it would. It came from nowhere. At first it's just way there at the back of my head like something come loose and floating down. I can tell when it going to happen. That don't mean I can stop it, though. And I'd known even when I was running, as if I could outrun it, knowing all the time that I couldn't. It floated down on me and even the feeling was one I hated, before the thing started. All my skin seemed touchy and things started in to move. And the lights coming through the tree branches were more than I could take. I held one hand with the other, knowing it wouldn't make a difference, had never made a difference so long as it had been happening. And it didn't now. The shaking started and then ran down me like a wave washing over and I could feel things going black and the shakes started in and then I was gone, gone wherever I went when it happened and everything washed away for a while. I don't know how long it took, have never known. I just come to and I'm sweating and my teeth hurt and I feel for my tongue and I open my eyes as if I just been born. Then it over and whatever washed over me has washed away and I'm left like a fish on the river bank, flopping around and wondering whatever happened to me that I'm there.

The dark came on suddenly and a flash of lightning lit everywhere up so it looked real scary. And then the thunder came, right over me as it seemed. There was no rain, though, and I thought maybe it would pass on by. But it didn't and the thunder came right on in after the lightning so that I knew it must have been most overhead. And then I began to think of twisters and how they might come right on through and flatten everything. But I guess I didn't really care about that. What did I care if I was killed? My daddy had been killed as well. But I got up and started forward and made my way all right, recognizing things, I guess, though I don't know how.

After a bit, I come into a clearing and saw the house. It were his right enough. There were no lights, so I went over by the window and crouched down. I could hear a noise coming from inside, a kind of whimpering like you hear from a wounded animal, that and a snoring sound. The windows were open but the screens were in place, except on one window that was closed. Just then the rain began, only it wasn't rain but hail that danced and jumped white across the ground. I figured there was no sense in staying outside. If I needed to see this man, I had best get indoors. Later, it didn't seem such a good idea, but I guess I wasn't thinking straight. If I had been thinking straight, I wouldn't have been there at all. Truth was, I was good and scared. I was scared over what had happened. I was scared because I couldn't speak. And I was scared because here I was outside the house of a white man, which was a quick way to get shot in the head, only my daddy had said that this was the man who had tried to stop them, even if he hadn't. I am trying to figure why I opened the window but, whatever it was, I opened it. I eased the window up, slipped inside, and slid it down again. I just sat on the floor for a bit, listening to the hail outside, listening to it beating on the roof, and listening, too, to the sounds of the man in the next room.

Then I began to think how he would wake up and shoot me dead. And I stood up, not sure what to do. I knew I should have left then, opened that window and got myself out, but there was something else in me, someone whispering in my ear and saying to go in and see this man.

So I went in. It were dark so that I couldn't see anything except the doorway. I stepped through and stood there, waiting for the lightning to flash, and, when it did, I got to see him. He were lying there, his eyes closed but puffed up and scraped as if someone had thrown him off a truck. There was a smell, just a human smell, I guess, but it were different. Then it were dark again. A minute later, it flashed and I could see something strange about his chest. I didn't like what I was seeing and it sounded as if he were on his way to being dead and I had seen enough of that. I went back into the other room and nearly tripped over a chair. I sat down on it and didn't know what to do. I never been so scared. Then the lightning flashed again and I see his gun, leaning up against the wall. And for a bit I thought that maybe I should take it in and shoot him like they shot my daddy. He were white. It were others like him done this thing. But then I remembered he weren't like that and I began to think how he was all smashed up and how maybe that was because he had helped my daddy, so I didn't do nothing. I just sat there, with a bundle of things in my hand, and waited for morning to come. I didn't know what I would do when morning came, but I figured maybe I would know by then or maybe he would wake up and tell me what to do.

I guess I fell asleep, because the next thing I knew it were light and he was walking in through the doorway. He didn't see me at first. He looked real scary and walked as if he was trying to hold hisself together. Then he just stops and looks at me and I looked back and I knew that whatever I did, he weren't going to kill me, mostly because he didn't look as if he could, but also because if he got smashed up like that for my daddy, why was he going to do bad to me? So I just looked back at him and after a bit he walked on through and out the back. I could see how there was an outhouse out there and I guessed he was gone to that. Then I realized that I needed to go as well, but I just sat there because there was no way I could go out while he was there.

After a bit, he came back in. He asked me who I was, but I couldn't answer. I didn't have no voice to answer and I just looked back at him until all of a sudden he half-turns around and hits the ground as if he wants to come on out the other side. Whatever they'd done to him had broken something inside. I looked at him and thought maybe I should be on my way. Anyone find me in there and him on the ground, a gun to hand, and I would be dead enough. But I figured this were the man who had tried to save my daddy and I couldn't leave him lying there.

I tried to lift him, but he were too heavy. He were making a strange noise as well, so that I was afraid again that he might be going to die. I went in the other room and found some cloth to cover him. Then, when I heard him begin to stir, I found a cup in the sink and dipped it in a pail. The water smelt of the earth.

Later, he got hisself up, though I don't know how, and went through in the other room. He hadn't been there but a second than he fell down so that I had to pull him into bed. I had to drag him, putting my hands under him. He groaned and made strange noises and I could hardly look at his chest where it was all burnt and swole up. I had to climb up on the bed, all smeared with red and black from his blood. Then I pulled until I fell over backwards, but I got him up there and then moved him about. The storm was still on outside and it seemed that the roof would lift up. There were no light to see by except the lightning that made everything milk white and then all dark again.

He woke at last and stared at me like he wanted to kill me, except he could hardly move. I went out and catched a rabbit. I found where they was and just sit there with a rock. There was no time for no snare so I waited and was lucky with the first throw. I twisted its neck and then tied some line around it and took it inside. There was no way he could do anything. He was half asleep and half just rambling. He kept talking to me but there was no way I could say nothing to him. My voice had gone and though it frightened me, I guess, more than anything, there was nothing I could do.

I had never been near no white man before, leastways not this close. His skin weren't white but grey, where it weren't red and purple from where it was swole up. There was a smell. It were part burnt skin and part something else. I skinned the rabbit and found a potato and carrot, mouldy and rubbery, but cooking would get rid of that. I had ate plenty of mouldy vegetables and they never did me no harm.

I fed him some because he didn't seem to have no strength. And I wondered again what I was doing here. I had done better to have done what my daddy said. And maybe they didn't care nothing about me. I guess it was him they was mad at. But here I was and I didn't want to go on out there, not while the storm was on.

If things hadn't happened the way they did, I guess I would have waited a day or some and then took off where I should have gone in the first place. But the men come. He were off in the outhouse while I sat in the kitchen. The sun were up and I was thinking it were about time for me to be going. I saw him come out and start on back. Then he just stopped as though he had been shot. He stopped and looked across somewhere I couldn't see. So I went in the other room and looked out the window. And there were two of the men that did what they did to my daddy. They were standing there with they rifles and I figured they had come for me and that the white man would hand me over. But I seen what they done and weren't no way I was going to let that happen. I had seen his gun. And I had seen where he kept his shells. So I went back in the kitchen and picked out a couple of shells. I guess my hand was shaking and I had trouble getting them in, though I had shot some before. My uncle had had a gun before he lost it in trading at the store. I knew how the shells went in. Even so, with my hands shaking it were difficult. At last they were in and I closed up the gun.

I could see from the way he was looking that they were circling round. I didn't know where to go and what I were going to do. I figured I'd just stand there and, when they came for me, fire the gun before they fired theirs. Then I heard what they was saying. They cut across the doorway, talking to the man, to my man who I had fed on rabbit stew, and they didn't look behind them because they were fixed directly on him. And I realized then that they were going to kill him like they killed my daddy. And when they had killed him, they would kill me, so I moved to the doorway not knowing what I was meant to do.

When they started in to rush him, it were just like they'd done to my daddy and I guess it was as if I had the chance all over again to save him or at least to get those that had hanged and then shot him. I brought the gun up right away and fired. The one I was pointing at seemed to fly forward. The man, my man, saw me right off. His eye slid right past the other man and took in where I was standing and that I had his gun. Then the other man swung around toward me and I fired so that he dropped down to the ground as well. I had never shot at no one before and them dropping down like that seemed like a dream. If I had had another shell, I don't know that I wouldn't have shot the other man and finished it all right there, but I didn't and he came across to me and took the gun out of my hand. He walked right on past and never said a thing. Then, a moment later, he come out again and went over to one of them on the ground and shot him. He had been moaning some. I guess he shot him like you would a wounded bird. Either way, he shot him. Then he turns around and says how we would have to get out of there or they would catch us, them others, or the law. And I saw where that was right and how there was nothing to do now but get away from there, though where we could go I couldn't think. With the law on us, it didn't seem to me there was anywhere we could go. They would get us for sure and kill us both. Just a few hours since I were weeding the garden. Now I was dead for sure and I had killed two men, one if you didn't count the one he shot, because I guess he were still alive. But the thing that cut right through me and that I couldn't let go of was that my daddy was dead and I had done nothing to stop it. But I guess that meant nothing to the man who grabbed ahold of my arm and told me to get out of there with him. Which is how come I was running through the woods and into the ice-cold stream with a white man who looked like the Devil hisself.

~

He moved on forwards. The path was narrow and he could see it wasn't used by much more than fishermen. He kept to the side at first, thinking that maybe those following, as following he was sure they would be, might not notice. Then he thought of the dogs and walked in the middle. No good dog can be fooled for long and the woods were full of the best. There were those who would sooner lose their kin than lose their dog, knowing that good dogs are rare and people keep spilling out if you just do the right thing. Every now and then he looked behind to see if the boy was keeping up, but he had come to believe that he was tough enough. Not many would do what he had done, none as far as he knew, knowing none of that kind.

He knew the railroad was ahead but not how far, and he hadn't begun to think what he might do when he reached it. He had never ridden the rails himself, never stirred more than a few miles from where he had been born, not imagining that any place else was any better and perhaps not any worse neither. When his wife had spoken of Birmingham or New Orleans, she wasn't speaking of places she knew but of other places where perhaps things was different. But unless different was better, why would anyone travel to them? Besides, he had told her, what was there for him to do in such a place? Here, at least, there was work from time to time. Here was familiar and there is something to be said for familiar places. So they settled for what they had got only to discover that they didn't have anything at all. The Bible says it, he had been told by the preacher at her funeral. God gives to them that have and takes from those that haven't even that which they have. And that had seemed about right to him, not in the sense that that was the way things ought to be but in the sense that that was the way he had always found them to be, not expecting different, either. Except, he guessed, that in marrying he had forgotten for a while, thought that things might be changed, knowing deep down, as it seemed to him now, that they never could be and never would.

After a while, the path disappeared as if whoever followed it simply turned around or dove into the river and he wondered whether he might not do the same. But this was all secondary growth, not too difficult to get through, so that he thought to keep on yet awhile.

Then he stopped. He had heard something, or felt something.

'You hear that?'

They both stood listening. The boy looked around him as if looking could help him hear, which of course it can.

'Hear that?'

The boy looked at him and shook his head.

It had been a long way off and indistinct, but it was a sound he knew, a sound he was used to hearing in the distance.

'Dogs,' he said.

The boy's eyes widened.

'Doesn't mean they after us. Seems too soon to me. The woods are full of dogs. Some let out on their own to do mischief, others hunting things down. We come aways. It too soon for them to be after us.'

Even so, he shifted the gun into his other hand and set off between the trees, by no means as clear in his mind as he had appeared to the boy. The sound of the dogs was what he had been waiting for.

The sun was low in the sky now and shadows had begun to link the trees together in a tangle of darkness. He went still faster, almost breaking into a run.

'Keep up!' he shouted over his shoulder, not bothering to look around, knowing that the boy would be there, had no choice but to be there any more than he did. And as he ran, so the pain began to seep back into him again, his shirt rubbing against his chest, his hand alive, throbbing where he had to use it to carry the gun, switching it from the other hand when it was too much to bear. Then he stopped and, though he tried not to, sank to his knees. He had thought he was better, but no one recovers from that, assuming them to have suffered it, by simply walking away, running away from it. He wasn't just running from the dogs and maybe the men who were with them, but from everything that had happened and that was now spelled out on his body, and not just in the letter burnt in his flesh by those who wanted his flesh to shout out to the world what they would make him if not what he was. It was spelled out in what it had taken from him, beyond his pride. He was weak. Only the day before, it had been an effort to move from one room to another. Now he had swum and run and walked and run and he knew suddenly, and without any possibility of denial, that he could not walk another step.

The boy stood beside him, waiting for him to rise, and he struggled to do so, but his legs simply gave way and he fell sideways. Though the day was ending, the air was still liquid. The heat took whatever energy he had left and he lay down flat, letting his arms drop by his side.

'Listen,' he whispered, so that the boy had to lean forward, resting a hand by his head and pressing his ear to his lips. 'Listen for the dogs.'

The boy did as he was told, standing still and trying to sort out the noise of a dog from the other noises that created the music of the woods. But he could hear nothing beyond the everything. He knelt by the man again and shook his head. The man nodded and passed out where he lay, as though the news gave him permission, his head settling in last year's leaves.

When he woke, the moon was high and silver and the woods were transformed. He felt cold and alone. For a second, he could no more remember where he was than he could his own name. It was as if he were reborn and expected to make himself up as he went along. He turned his head, stiff from lying in a single position. He could just make out the boy, squatting on his haunches still, as if he were sleeping that way, as perhaps they did, he knowing nothing of their ways. Up above, through a gap in the trees, he could see a swathe of stars sprinkled like pepper. The moon was a sliver, a fingernail, but its light was a kind of grace spread over the world. It reminded him of a picture he had seen in the church: shepherds on a hill, dark, picked out against a glow of white. Then he recalled where he was and listened, listened for the dogs, but beyond the croaking frogs and rasping crickets could hear nothing. Still he listened, his body tense, but there was nothing that said pursuit, that said men and guns and rope and fire.

'Boy,' he said, softly, though why softly he could not have said, except perhaps not to change the noise of the woods so that others might detect the change.

The boy stayed where he was.

'Boy.'

Still the boy stayed where he was until, at last, he picked up a stick and walked across to him. He did not crouch down again, but stood there a second and then cleared the soil with his foot, brushing aside the leaves and smoothing the soil. Then he took the stick and wrote. The soil was dark on top but light underneath and as he wrote so the letters stood out white in the moonlight. He wrote his name with the stick, having been 'boy' for long enough, perhaps. He wrote slowly and the man watched the letters appear one by one: 'James.'

'So,' said the man, 'your name's Jim.'

The boy shook his head violently and with the stick underlined the name he had written.

'James, your name's James.'

He nodded.

'All right. If it's James, that's what I'll call you. A person's got a right to a name. Only thing he has got a right to. Well, James, I guess we wait till sun-up. Get yourself some sleep because I doubt you'll get any for a while. I don't know if they behind us or not. If they ain't now, they will be soon enough. I don't hear no dogs and I wasn't expecting to hear none yet, but it don't pay to be surprised. You understand what I'm saying?'

The boy understood, or so it seemed, for he stood off a pace or two and then settled down right where he was, scraping together some leaves and using a root with a fallen branch laid on it for a pillow.

For all he had told the boy to sleep, the man himself lay staring up at the sky, trying to get his mind to understand how it could go on for ever, with no beginning and no end and what the connection might be between such a spread of time and his own life, how he was in mortal danger and nothing out there gave a damn whether he lived or died. He had heard how what he was seeing was from the past, how the light that flowed over his hand had left wherever it came from thousands of years before. It was a link to a world gone by, and not a world like the one he knew because it came from some other place stranger than any he could imagine. Unless there was a God out there. His folks had gone to church when he was young, had gone regular, and were against sin, which seemed to be everywhere, so that he was forever being hollered out or clipped round the head for committing it. But it had gone from his life, that God, and not only when his wife and son died, neither. It had gone somewhere along the way without him even noticing it. Church dropped away, then prayers, then everything that was left except this sense of wondering what it was all about when the sky was a smear of stars and every now and then you saw one shoot across like a fallen angel.

A cloud scudded across the thin moon, enfolding him for a moment in darkness, though he could still make things out in the starlight, as though that would be enough if the moon should ever fail. Then it was gone again and he shivered as a milky light washed over his hands and made him look as if he was already dead. It was the colour his wife had looked when she gave up at last and breathed out that breath that she had stored for so long. The boy was there somewhere, but who was he? No, he was alone; the boy meaning nothing. He was all alone and with everything taken from him he had ever owned. He drifted into sleep at last, floating on a white lake which rippled slowly in a breeze, and where the ripple creased the silk water, it was dark as if the depths beneath were eternal night, a spill of black ink where God dipped his pen to write the names of the doomed.

He jolted into consciousness with the sun on his face. The boy was holding out a root to him.

'What time is it?' he asked, forgetting that neither one of them had a watch and that one of them lacked a voice. 'What's that?'

The boy held it out. He took it and held it to his nose. It smelt bitter. He tasted it. It was sweet. He saw that the boy was eating it and bit a piece of it off. It was fibrous but it reminded him that he was hungry and, with no food to hand, he swallowed.

'We gotta go. Come on.'

He got up, in doing so standing on the name the boy had scratched the night before. The light soil had darkened during the night and he could not have made out the name if he had tried, but his mind was on other matters.

'Let's go.' He threw the root in the bushes, not trusting anything he did not know.

Again he led the way. From the angle of the sun, he realized that it was later than he would have liked. Up ahead there was the makings of a path and on an impulse he followed it. It was narrow and he could not think who would have made it. He thought that maybe it was some animal but there were no tracks that he could see. So it was just a path for no reason, but in taking it maybe he gave it one. After half an hour or so, it brought him back to the river, but he was confident he had not come in a circle. The river itself meandered back and forth, bending back on itself as if reluctant to go anywhere at all, as if looking for a way to slow itself down.

'Perhaps we should have stayed with it,' he said, half to himself, knowing that he would not have survived the cold but remembering its power to kill his pain. The trees fell back some, forming a kind of clearing. There were rocks, which was why no trees had rooted themselves, but the rocks were surrounded by river moss, almost olive green and springy to the foot. He looked around, not welcoming open ground, but everything seemed still and there were no sounds of the dogs that were to be his warning.

They were halfway across when the bullet took him clean

through the shoulder. He was no more than half a dozen paces from the river and it knocked him toward it. He knew he had been hit, but felt nothing. He recovered himself, not thinking, at first, what had hit him, looking for the boy as if he might have punched him for no reason at all, his brain trying to make sense of the messages coming in. As a result, he stood waiting for the next shot, not thinking to do anything, not thinking to run or surrender, not knowing, even, that it was a shot. And there was another, but as it rang out he was already falling into the river, the boy's arms around his waist, his weight knocking him backwards into the rush of water. Then he was under that water. It closed about him. The shock of the cold brought him back to full consciousness, as he turned to shake the boy's arms from him, afraid he would drown who should instead have been worried about the bullet the boy had saved him from. Except that his brain would still not register the bullet, only the boy who seemed intent to wrestle him to death, who sought his life as perhaps he had a right to believe he should. And everything moved slowly, as if he had all the time in the world, time to figure it out, all that had happened from the very beginning, time to free himself from the boy who took him down to his death.

They did break surface, the boy and he, but the speed of the river had carried them free of the clearing and out into the centre. He caught sight of something, someone, a dark movement back there on the bank, but was under water again, pulled down this time not by the boy but by a current that seemed to wrap itself around him and tug at him as if it was time for him to die, and not by a bullet either.

And he was cursing himself for not pushing on the way that he knew that he should, figuring, at last, what had happened and understanding, in that instant, that they had looped around him and cut back from the bridge as he knew that they must, all this while turning and tumbling, calm inside, knowing that this was death and that all he could do was submit. No thought for the boy, who was flown out of his life, the life that was ending. And so he tumbled, aware that he was turning and hitting rocks and being drawn forwards and down and around in all directions at ever greater speed. He saw flashes of silver light edged with blue and then the clean dark of the river bottom, end over end, and no time to breathe, no need to breathe, either.

And indeed the river did run faster as it narrowed and cut through a gorge so that it was a froth of white with furrowed water like a tongue folded on itself to hawk a spit and parts where it spun off in separate whirlpools, the whirlpools themselves rushing on and down, finding their own way, with wills of their own.

But he didn't die, being simply rushed forwards and along like any other piece of flotsam fallen into the river and spun and dipped and sashayed. The river swept under the bridge, the bridge where he had meant to jump a train and take himself away from this place toward somewhere else where he could be free. It swept underneath and out round a bend that slowed it some, then back on itself like a snake edging ahead using the curves of its body, going ahead by going sideways.

He didn't die but instead kept hitting the surface and drawing in air with a rasping sound he couldn't hear, what with the rush of the river and the tumble of thoughts going through his mind. He was using lives faster than a cat. First the burning, when he thought they would string him up for sure, and then the two outside his home, seeking him out, then getting hit when he thought they were hours behind, and now drowning. Well, someone was trying to tell him something right enough.

And he smiled to himself, even in the midst of all this, and the smile told him that he wasn't going to die and indeed he realized that the river was losing some of its force or that he was being pulled off to where it was quieter and his face was clear of the water and he was breathing almost easy now.

When he came to land, he was drifting slowly. He could see where the main body of the water was still sweeping by, with branches and debris from the storm like so many creatures bobbing up and down. Then there was ground beneath his feet and he was pulling himself forwards where a fan of bushes came down almost to the water's edge. There was no pain from his shoulder. Indeed, he had almost forgotten where he had been hit, but he was used by now to what the cold could do to ease pain until the thaw set in. He thought about the boy, as he hadn't from the moment he first hit the water, and remembered being hit by him just after he was hit by something else, thinking for a split second that it was the boy that had done it and was trying to finish him off, but recalling, too, as it seemed to him now, the sound of the shot, the first and a second just before the two of them went in together. But he was nowhere now. Not that he could see. He looked out at the river, but he must have been swept on past. If they had gone in together, they would have sailed along together, died together, lived together. There was no sign of him, though, and he figured he must be dead as he was convinced he should be himself, seeing he had taken so much punishment and hadn't swum a stroke, just been drawn along as if his life wasn't his to live any more, just like a twig in a torrent taken wherever the torrent had it in mind to go. So the boy was gone. He thought no more than that, lying gasping, a fish on the river bank, waiting for death.

Then he thought of the men. He had no sense of how far he had come or how long it had taken, this ride of his on an ice-water train. And train was the word in his head, though it took him a moment to remember why. How far away was that now, and how far the men? He turned on his back and looked around. Behind him, and through the trees, he could see the end of the bridge, up where the land rose above the river. Having no clear idea how close he had been when they caught him, he could still not figure where they might be, though he knew that the bends must have folded space, bringing him back toward them in sweeping him away.

He eased himself up and felt a sharp pain, clean and clear, in his shoulder. He looked down and could see a neat hole in his shirt. He pulled it back and there it was, punched through flaccid white skin, with no trace of blood. He reached his other hand over his shoulder and down and found another hole, not as neat and small but reassuringly there. It was through and out and with luck time would deal with that. He needed the boy, though, recalled the moment in the wood, with the silver of moonlight, when he wrote his name in the dirt.

He shook his head, alarmed that his mind was wandering. He was about to make the same mistake again, lie around when they were coming toward him. There had been no dogs, that's what had fooled him, or if there were, they had been well-enough trained to keep quiet. And if he didn't hear them the first time, he wouldn't the second. They might be crazy, those men, breeding up in the family so that they went bad as animals will go bad if you breed them up the same way, but they were cunning and sly and trained their dogs well so that though there were those wouldn't give them the time of day, those same people would pay them for one of their dogs that would do what they were told but had the instincts to go on their own and find whatever it was they had to find.

And it wasn't the law. The law didn't just shoot you down. It might do just about anything else, but it wouldn't do that, so he knew what he was up against and that made him feel better in some way he could not explain to himself, still less to others if he had been put to it.

He thumped his balled fist on his leg. His mind was wandering again when his body should have been on the move. He looked around for the boy, scanned the far bank in case he had been dropped there, as though the river were a crow dropping carrion from the sky. There was nothing there, nothing you could call a boy. Not that he acted like a boy. Not that he acted like a nigger. Well, you took people as they were. Most he didn't take at all, preferring to live on his own without the complication. He punched himself again, bringing himself back to what he must do.

Luckily the shoulder wound was on the same side as his burnt hand, so he could lever himself up with the other, crouching low in case they were out there waiting to put a round clear through his head. He listened, but it was useless so close to the river. All he could hear was the drawing rush of water and the squawk of a bird or two close by.

The bushes gave cover. So close to the water, they were deep green and tall so he could almost stand, though not quite, so that he had to move forwards like an old man might, bent a little, shuffling through the undergrowth. But which way to go? The bridge was where they were coming from, maybe where they would stake themselves out, waiting for him to come to them. Then he realized that the gun had gone. He had known it all along, except that it had never surfaced in his mind. He had a picture of himself falling into the river, pushed there by the boy, with his gun flying off out of his hand, his arm flung out as if the water were the ground and he had to protect himself from hitting it. It was not the side that took the round. Even so, he had let it go so that the shells in his pocket were useless now and he had nothing to go against them with. He thought to throw them away in disgust, disgust at himself for letting go, but there seemed no point. Besides, maybe there was a chance he might get it back or even another. That was how his mind was working and he smiled again at his own foolishness in thinking such.

He decided on the bridge because he couldn't think what else to do. If he kept on going, they would catch him for sure, slowed down as he was and with no one to help him now. Whatever the danger, the railroad was the only way out. Even granted that they were up there waiting for him, it was better to go that way where there was still some chance, no matter how small, than that other where there was none at all, except just keeping ahead of them for a few more hours, running yourself ragged like a deer that knows no better, that doesn't know it makes no difference how long you run because the dogs will get you and a bullet can move faster than you run. He had been told once. Fire a rifle parallel to the ground and the bullet will hit the ground a mile off before the shell case hits it by your feet. That's how inevitable a bullet is. You don't get to dodge them, like in the movies.

The bushes gave way to trees which cut down on the cover but made it easier to move. The land was sloping up already and he had to keep in mind where the bridge was, now that it was out of sight. Also, he was beginning to feel his shoulder. As he moved, so he heated up and was glad the round had gone clean through or he might have lost the shoulder out here where there was no one to treat it. And as he thought that, he realized that he was thinking of surviving. With the warmth came the pain, but with the pain came a new confidence. They might be cunning but they weren't over-bright. And perhaps they had had no time for the dogs. They had come so fast that maybe there was just the men themselves, or even just the one of them. After all, the two at his home had had no dogs. So maybe there was just the one, come on ahead, confident he could track them, taking a chance on where he was heading and swinging ahead as he would have done if he hadn't had to keep out of sight.

It was steeper than he had thought and the cold had left him numb. His skin had started to pink up. He was maybe halfway up when he looked back where he had come, looked back to the river and saw the bank just beyond where he had got out himself. And it seemed to him, suddenly, that there was something there, lying like a slug maybe, where the bushes thinned. He tried to make out what it might be, knowing already what it was. He had missed him because of the bushes, because he hadn't wanted to take time to look around. But it was him all right, the boy, lying there, dead maybe, dead for a certainty because if it was a miracle that he could have walked away, it would have been a double miracle for them both to have walked away, baptized and risen again.

And now he stood there, not knowing what he should do. Time was everything. If he could reach the bridge before they did, not knowing how far he had come or how long ago they had watched him fly through the air into a river they maybe thought had drowned him, maybe there was still a chance. Thing was, he didn't know how long he had. Then that thought caught up with him. Why would they think he had survived? The river was as wild as he had seen it. The storm had swollen it so it looked alive, and they had seen him take the bullet. Maybe they would reckon him dead, call it evens, be on their way. He knew right away it was false. They would need to see the body, need to carry it back to show they had done what they set out to do. There was no getting away from them as easy as that.

To go back for the boy would be suicide. His one hope was to make for the railroad. And besides, he was dead, or looked such just lying there. But he had lain there himself and here he was on a hillside and hurting like hell. He stood, undecided, knowing deep down what he was going to do but having no reason for doing it. What was the point? Why would he do that? And then he was descending, as he knew he would, heading back to the last place he should have gone, down toward the river where they would be looking for him if they weren't waiting for him up above, if they weren't watching him even now and lining up their sights to finish the job. Even so, he went on down, walking easier going down. He came to the bushes and crouched, though it wouldn't do any good because the boy was out in the open. Even so, he crouched as if he were an Indian tracker, until he came to where the scrub died back and the boy lay limp on the ground.

The first thing he did was to take hold of him with his good hand and drag him back into the bushes. Time enough to see if he was dead when they weren't out there where they would be dead in a second if there was anyone to see. He pulled him face down, his legs digging two trenches in the soft mud, trenches that might be seen from above, though who would have known them for what they were, trenches dug by the feet of a dead boy? Except he wasn't dead, or not quite, it seemed. He flipped him over on to his back and knelt down beside him as if offering a prayer.

His eyes were closed and his neck seemed to flop over when he turned him, like a hen caught for the pot. He was unsure how to tell whether life had left him or not, whether he had breathed in the cold water so that his veins were full of death.

He crouched down and put a finger on his neck, not knowing where to feel, not knowing whether the faint pulse he felt was in his finger or the boy's body. He leaned forward, putting his wrong hand to the ground and pulling back suddenly, hugging the hand to him as though it were a baby to be comforted. Then he leaned forwards again, his ear to the boy's mouth, as if he could hear anything as quiet as a breath with the river running by. Then something welled up in his own throat, a kind of smothering feeling of urgency. He knelt up again and put both hands underneath, easing him over, despite the pain that shot through hand, chest and shoulder. He turned his face so that it was no longer staring down into the earth's core, and sat astride him, pushing down with both hands, though one hand felt like fire and the bruise of his broken ribs pressed into him with each downward pressure. He had seen it done before, not done it himself but watched as they tried to bring a child back to life in the Fishers' pond, pressing down as though they were pushing it into its grave, as well they might have been since that was where it went the following day. He pressed down and watched the lips to see if the water would vomit up. And after a while that was what it did, like a pump lifting water from the still, black depths. But still no sign of life. He flipped him over and thumped him with his good hand, thumped him hard between the shoulder blades and then again, lower.

When a minute or three or four had gone by, he slid his hands underneath again and turned him so that he was on his back again. Then he leaned forward and put his mouth over the boy's mouth, his white mouth over the black mouth, to breathe his own life into the boy as if sharing might redeem him, though if asked he could not have said why he chose to share in this way. He breathed in and then lifted away, looking for a spark, listening for a sound. And at last one came, a sudden cough, an ooze of water and then another choke that seemed to start him into life like a truck teased into going when all thought it broken for ever.

And could he have done such a thing for his wife? The thought came to him even now, as he knelt in the mud by the side of a river, his mouth wet with a nigger's spittle. Could he have brought her back as he had this boy, taken the long sigh that ended her life and sighed it back into her so that his life would have been different and the world maybe, too? Why hadn't he thought to do it then? But the thought was gone in an instant, faded back into that dull regret where he stored everything he couldn't use but that wouldn't leave him alone until he found somewhere for it to go.

He lifted his leg back over him, easing away so that the boy would not know what he had done, waiting for him to open his eyes, confident, now, that he would do so, as he did, staring up into the blue sky and then letting his head fall to the side so that he could see the man who had brought him back to life, though he wouldn't know that was what he had done, neither then nor later, but simply imagine he had come to at last after crawling from the water he had no memory of entering until, after a moment or so more, he did feel again the shock of the cold and the old man's hands around him, pulling him down.

'We got to shift,' said the man, bending toward him as though sharing a secret. 'They still around. We got to be going.' He could see, though, that he would have to give him time, so he sat beside him and looked up at the hillside, watching for a flash of light or a sudden movement. He sat beside him until the boy's choking ended and he saw that his eyes had cleared.

They stood up, the boy and the man, the boy less steadily than the man, and began to retrace the steps the man had taken before he stopped and went back for the boy who was dead.

Again the ground lifted away from them so that they had to lean into it, neither of them fit for it now, having been battered against rocks and shown the gates of glory. They climbed, none the less, aching and pained, the boy damaged now, as the man had been, and both plunged into the same purging water.

The trees thinned out a little toward the top, so that there was no real cover once they had broken the skyline. Speed mattered more than anything, because once they were seen, there was nothing to be done. The man said nothing, figuring the boy was bright enough to understand the state of things, and they struggled side by side until at last they stepped out on to the edge of the railroad track where it shot out into space across the river. There was no one there. Not that he had expected them to be standing in view. They would be back in the trees, sighting along their rifles.

He pulled the boy back.

'Lie down. We got to wait till a freight comes along. Then we got to get on board. Only one chance, and me with an arm that's useless.'

It was no more than the truth, because how was he going to pull himself up and on to a wagon or into a box car with only one good arm? But thinking about it did no good. Some things you did when the time came because there was nothing else to do. Even so, he could see the difficulty of it and somehow speaking it aloud made it seem more real.

He wanted to edge out and lay his head on the line to see if he could hear the engine off in the distance, rumbling toward him, wheels turning, bearing down on the line; but it was too big a chance. Suppose the men weren't there before but were there now? How could it be worth the risk? To tell the truth, he was surprised they weren't there already, hitting him again with another round. But maybe that was the point. To watch him try and fail, or pick him off as he ran like a fool, imagining he could get away, him and the boy who they would like to get as much as him. More, even.

The heat was up and the air like molasses. It was an effort just to breathe in and out. The track itself was laid on white granite chips that dazzled and reflected so that the world seemed to waver and jump. He glanced across at the boy, who looked exhausted. He was the one that got hit. On the other hand, the boy got pulled back from the other side and that must have taken it out of him, he figured. Take the shine off the shine.

Then, in the distance, came a mournful cry, like a wolf crying for its mate. It was a train climbing the gradient, where the hill fell away toward the south. By the time it came to them, it would be going slow enough to get on board, if the boy had got his strength up and if his arm held out, as he doubted it would. He had fixed his mind on the train as the way out for them both, but it had been no more than an idea. Even the sound of it climbing the hill and a twanging from the rails as if it spoke to them didn't make it real enough to know he could make it. He nudged the boy.

'Wait till it level and then run beside it. Match your speed to it. You won't get but one chance. Odds are, the box cars will be closed, so try for the wagons. Make sure before you jump or you'll lose your legs. Don't care nothing about them others. They's there or they's not and ain't nothing neither you nor me can do about that. Our job is to climb aboard. And if you make it and I don't, you keep on going. Don't think nothing of me. Keep on going as long as you can. Put some space between this place and you. Ain't nothing for you here no more. Ain't nothing for me, neither.'

The words spilled out as though they had been stored away,

cascaded like water down a mountainside. And as he said it, so the truth of it came home to him for the first time. When he had left the cabin, he had thought that was the end. Now he realized he had been hanging on to something, just the same, though he couldn't say what that could be, except, perhaps, two graves that might open again on Judgement Day, the Judgement Day in which he was sure he did not believe. But the sight of the railroad lines and the sound of the engine closing in on him told him it was over. Telling the boy did it, too. He spoke to the boy, but he was speaking to himself.

The train swung into sight, the cow catcher on the engine like a splayed hand. It rocked from side to side under the effort of climbing the hill. It must have a long load, he thought, glad that he would have time to get on board if he could only manage it, feeling as he did, with a boy just wrung out from drowning. It pulled toward him, sun flashing on the windows of the engineer's cab as if they were eyes, searching him out. The whistle blew again, rising and falling, fading away like a memory. The road bed seemed narrow, suddenly, where he would have to run alongside, and, though he felt a surge of energy, his body preparing for what was to come, he knew, too, just how weak he was. So he was sure he knew he could never make it, the train rocking from side to side as it did like a ship at sea or a sailor on land. It closed on him, looking slow enough from where he was, head on or slightly to the side, shifting itself on the tracks as if it might leave them, roll right on over him where he lay. The clang of metal on metal receded into the distance, passed down the length of the train, like a message. Then it was beside him, looking large, towering above him. They were crouching down lest they be seen, close to the ground, hands flat on the granite chips. He had heard stories of men being beaten by conductors, tossed off if they made it or just as they tried, falling, sometimes, under the wheels, legs severed, hands sliced off. All this as he prepared. All this as the engine passed and the first of the wagons, hard iron on hard iron, and a breeze, suddenly, raising the dust. He wanted to lay there for ever, head down, eyes fast shut, telling himself he could stay where he was, knowing that if he did, it would be his grave. But then he was on his feet and tugging at the boy, feeling his weight at first, pulling him along, then letting go, and they were running. They had no more than two hundred feet or so before the track narrowed to take the bridge, narrowed so that there was no place to run but into the tangle of girders and struts, that or down again into the rushing cold of the river below and even that near impossible to do.

There was a flatbed beside him but no place to put his hand. He had thought, maybe, to try for where the wagons were coupled, but the coupling was set back, its parts clanging together so that anyone who tried would maybe be crushed to death. He ran beside it just the same, watched as it rocked and swung, metal buffer kissing metal buffer, pipes and cables hanging down. There was no more than a hundred feet now and he could feel his legs begin to go, that and an ache in his chest and shoulder both. A box car came level and he could see how the doors were open slightly, though there was no hand hold that he could detect. He had expected, maybe, a metal ladder, something to reach for, but there was nothing but this gap, swinging away and toward. The boy leaped ahead of him, turning so that he hooked a hand round the edge of the door, blocking him from jumping himself. Then, with a half-turn, he swung his legs up, supple with youth, like a fish flicking itself off into the gloom. Fifty feet and a pain in his chest. Fighting for air. No way to make it, as it seemed, no way to follow the boy whose legs disappeared as the wagon pulled away.

He glanced down at his feet, scared he would trip, looked ahead for the man with the gun he expected to step out in his path. Thirty feet, and the girders like so many arms reaching to embrace him. He jumped at last, risking everything on this, who had no choice to do otherwise, his feet slipping as he took off so that he grabbed lower than he wanted and grabbed with the arm that was shot through and burnt. He caught hold not with his hand but his elbow, bent round the door, his left hand, so that he was facing backwards, away from the direction it was going, his legs flying. Twenty feet.

The bridge was latticed with rusting girders, criss-crossed, a cat's cradle of iron, with space for a walking man but not for legs flying out as the train pulled free of the hill and on to the flat. He twisted himself, throwing his other hand back over his head, gripping the door with his one good hand, pulling as hard as he could, easing himself forwards. It was too late. The bridge was on him. He kicked his legs inward, seeking some purchase and found it where one of the planks of the wagon was broken. His toe jammed into it and the thrum of the girders pulsed in his ears as the shadows flickered and the note of the train changed. Down below, the river sparkled, but all he could see was the flaking brown paint of the slid-back door and the shadow of the girders blinking on and off, on and off. Then they were free and the train hit another gradient, slowing for a moment so that he could ease his foot out and pull on his one good hand. He felt another hand take hold of his jacket and ease him forwards. It was the boy, pulling against the motion of the train and making little difference but just enough to help him lever against the edge of the door and wriggle his chest around it, his burnt chest. It was the pain in the end that helped him do it, urged him on to one last effort.

It was round his waist now and he knew he was safe. He

rolled over and in and lay on his back, done, exhausted and destroyed, but in just the same. For a while, he thought of nothing, fighting for breath, one pain contending with another so that he seemed to glow with it, throb as the girders of the bridge had throbbed in his ears. He closed his eyes and everything glowed red, as though his blood were afire. The whistle of the train sounded as it gathered for its descent, proud it had made it, announcing itself to the world. It was some time before he gave any thought to the man with the gun, or the men, since he had no way of knowing how many there were. He wondered whether they had seen him jump aboard, he and the boy who was somewhere behind him in the gloom, thinking his own thoughts and fighting for air, too, if there was any justice in this world, as heaven knows there wasn't as far as he knew, travelling, now, from one place to another without knowing where that might be and him already changing, changed, indeed, so that he no more knew himself than the place he was headed. Both a mystery, like it was a mystery he had opened his mouth when he knew he should keep it shut, like it was a mystery he was travelling with a boy the colour of tar quite as if they were father and son, as God knows they might be kin in a place where no blood was pure, no matter what they said and how they acted, lynching their own, maybe, without knowing, without caring either.

~

I see the man who fired the shot. I looked across and see him in among the trees. I guess it was a flash of light or something, because he caught my eye. But no sooner I saw him than he fires and the white man takes it in the shoulder. We were by the river and the bullet pushed him to the edge. I looked back to the man and saw him lift the gun again and I knew we were both dead, so I jump for the river, taking the man along with me. The water ran fast and he clawed at me so that I had to kick free. Even so, I couldn't reach up to the air, though I see it above me, silver and blue. I hit my head on a rock which sprang me up to the top where I could take a breath, then I was spinning down again. After that, it was rocks and a spill of bubbles in my ears like bells and trying to keep clear and stay in the pull of the current. Then nothing, nothing until I looked up to see the white man bending over me and me lying on the river bank and choking water. I guess he got me out, but here he was already tugging at me and saying we got to climb a hill. They was after us still and we got to climb to the railroad track. And I knew it was true. I wanted to go off on my own, but I knew they would get me for sure, so I stayed with him and climbed the hillside, slipping where it was still slick from the rain.

I felt all bruised inside and on my back, and my face was rough like someone had rubbed it with dirt. Nothing stopped. Ever since the men came to the house, nothing had stopped. Things had happened one after another and there seemed no way I could hold them off. All we did was run and it didn't seem to make much difference whether we was in the water or on the land. There was people after us and no way I could see that they wouldn't get us. And I could see he were in a bad way and not likely to be much good. I could see where his gun had gone that I thought might be the saving of us like it was before, except that now it was gone and if they could shoot him once, they could shoot him again and me alongside him.

We reached the top and I could see how he was almost done. He was breathing heavy and favouring one side. He was shot up and knocked about so much, I was surprised he was moving at all. We lay down under the trees and looked down the track. I don't know how he knew anything would be along. I had heard the whistle before, right enough, but not so often I could be sure when anything would be along. Then, there it was, coming toward us. And he said how we should jump on board but not how we should do it. And he said that if I should make it I should keep on going, as if I would have thought to do anything else, though where I should go to he didn't say. Maybe he had somewhere to go, but I didn't. I did if I done what my daddy had said, but I didn't and had killed a man instead and so couldn't go there any more, as it seemed to me. So now I was travelling without knowing where.

I ran for the train, looking for where I could jump, and a car came along. I got in easy enough, though whatever happened to me in the river was making me feel bad. I turned around and there was the white man running beside the train, red in the face and panting like a bull. I looked and saw how the bridge was coming and thought he could never make it and how I would be alone after all, except he made this leap, old though he was, and I saw where his arm looped round the door, his hand reaching out as if there was something there he could take a hold of. And I could see it were the burnt hand and that the shoulder was the one he just got shot in so that I felt sure he would let go. His legs were flying and the bridge was pretty much on us. Then he must have managed it because the bridge was flicking by and he didn't get knocked off, so that as we cleared the bridge I reached out for his collar and managed to get him in.

I guess I did it for me and not for him. We were together now and there didn't seem anything I could do about it. I wouldn't have chosen to be with him, but there didn't seem anything else I could do. He could have left me by the river, given me up to them men, but he stuck there till I come to. And besides, he must know what to do. He a white man, after all.

He lay there and so did I. We were both tired through. We had got away. I just lay back on the floor among the straw and the dirt. There was nothing in the wagon but a heap of rags over in the corner. We were picking up speed now and easing down the hill. I could see the trees flickering by, so that after a bit I couldn't watch. The flickering made my head ache and I could feel that feeling that told me the shakes were coming. When I got that feeling, I had to make sure I were safe, so I pulled back from the doorway. I wanted to tell him, so he would know what to do, but I couldn't speak and couldn't think how to show him. And besides, maybe the feeling would go away. It sometimes did, especially if I could just lie still. Except that the wagon was rocking from side to side and the flashes of light from the doorway seemed to set my head to throbbing. I thought maybe to shut the door, but didn't trust myself to stand or get close to it. So there was nothing for it but to lie back and try to stop it from happening, though, if it wanted to, there wasn't nothing I could do, not a thing in the world. And the train was the same. It was going north, that much I knew, but where it was going I didn't know and anyway wasn't nothing to be done about that neither. It would just take me wherever it wanted to. And then the shakes came and the dark rose up, and I'm falling down into it like there is nothing but dark and I feel the shakes before it swallows me up. And then I am gone and not there no more, just somewhere where nobody is but a picture broken all to pieces. And then it was dark again and there was no me at all.

~

Something was over. A line had been drawn. He was tireder than he had ever been. There was no one pain, no one ache, his body simply hummed with pain and ache. Until now, he had thought of nothing but the train, as if the train were a destination in itself, except that he knew it wasn't. For the moment, though, it would do. It was putting distance between him and those who wanted him dead and who, if they knew he was on the train, as doubtless they would, could not possibly know where he would get off, since he didn't himself. For the first time, he felt if not at peace then relaxed, not tensed to fight or to run. Outside the door, the land was pulling away behind him, cutting by, each passing tree a second further off in time and space. Most of his life, nothing much happened each day that was any different from any other. He would work if there was work and not if there wasn't. Every now and then, he would go to the store or hunt in the wood, but nothing much marked off one time from another. Now things came at him one after another. It seemed to him that there was no rest. It was as though everything had been stored up and was now pouring out so fast that he could do nothing more than watch, as if it wasn't his life at all. Now here he was, heading north or thereabouts with his body all broken up and a bullet through his shoulder. He held out his hands as though he could catch the water that was his life, but it spilled right on through, sparkling but lost.

Thinking of it brought back the pain, or maybe it was the other way about. He reached up his finger to touch the wound but stopped short. It had gone clean through. Chances were, it would heal on its own. He had been shot before, when he was six and someone had fired a rifle across a field. It went through his hand, almost plumb in the middle. There was a scar there still. His mother had looked at him strange when he showed her the wound, punched through in the middle of his hand. It had healed right up with doctoring, though. Things happen. In the season especially, things could get real dangerous. He remembered a neighbour, walking with a boy on his shoulder. Someone way off took a shot at a squirrel and took the boy right between the eyes. His father had gone on walking, not realizing at first, except that the boy had slumped forward, playing, as he thought, until the blood come down on his face. He remembered how the man had run along, holding the boy out in front of him, not running anywhere since there was nowhere to run to, just like a chicken will run when its head is off, looking for the head, maybe, or figuring it can outrun its own death. A clean shot through the shoulder maybe wasn't so bad, not when you thought what it might have been.

He heard a sudden sound behind him, not a sound he had heard before. It was the boy. He was lying on the floor of the car, kicking his heels, shaking all over like a badly tuned car. Everything was shaking. For a second, the man sat there, trying to make sense of what he was seeing, the boy lost in some other world. He swung up and went across to him. His face was screwed up and his body had begun to arch. Not knowing what to do, he did nothing, thinking maybe that the boy was mad or had got hit and they hadn't known it, a hit in the head maybe. There was spittle around his lips so that he thought maybe he had got bit by something with the madness, a dog perhaps. That he had seen, or heard rather, the scream in the wood, and, finally, a shot that nobody asked about, knowing it was all a father could do for a boy got bit by a dog should have been put down itself, was put down but too late to save the one it bit.

Then it was gone and the boy relaxed, sank back down, his eyes closed, his head on one side. Something had gone out of him. Whatever devil had been inside had come out. He put his ear to the boy's chest. He was breathing. He was breathing fast but, even as he listened, that breathing became regular as though he were asleep, as perhaps he was. Then he realized it was just a fit, would have realized earlier, he guessed, but for everything else that had happened, but for his own pain and confusion. He had seen it once before in a woman who fell down at the church. People had thought she had seen a vision, but it was just a fit. But seeing it before didn't mean he knew what to do. He guessed, indeed, that there was nothing to do except let it take its course, like it had done. It was a good thing, he thought, that the boy had taken sick away from the doorway and that thought got him to thinking. What if he had had a fit plunging down the river or climbing the hill or when two men had been pointing guns at him and it was the boy who rescued him, whatever his reason for doing it? And what must it be like never to know when you would be taken? How you might be leaning over the fire or riding a horse or just about anywhere when suddenly God reaches down a finger and pushes you off so that you woke up burnt or broken or didn't wake at all. Wasn't it bad enough he had been born black? Now, along with that, he was cursed with the fits. He turned away, content to leave him where he lay, and went back to the doorway where the woods had given way to open country and he could see the odd cow or two, stationary in flying fields.

~

They was lying right out in front. I didn't see them first. I was looking to see if there was anyone there. Never thought anything like that. When I got close, I could see how Tom had got shot in the back and Mikey twice. Must have been two'n them. One person couldn't have got off the shots, not in the time they had. I picked up the rifles and shucked the slugs. Hadn't been fired, near as I could tell. I did it instead of looking at Tom and Mikey. Who'd have thought that nigger-loving bastard'd do this. Should've strung him up when we had the chance.

I kicked the door in, knowing they wouldn't be there but crouching down in case they was. Some kind of smell around the place. The dogs run in ahead of me but didn't find nothing. Nothing there to find, turns out. Two'n them been there, though. Two cups, two bowls. I always thought he were alone. Never seen him with no one in all those years, not that I gave him any mind. Who would've thought he'd be what he was. Truth was, I didn't believe it neither. Them two at the store is a couple of Jews, it always seemed to me. No credit and looking out of the sides of they eyes. And who would want to touch her? Even a nigger would pass on that. All the same, though. Can't let anyone get away with nothing or there'd be no end to it. And now where were we but Tom and Mikey dead? I still couldn't see how that could have happened. I crouched down and looked out through the window, as if they might've got up. But they was still there, one shot in the back, one twice in the front from up close, the shot not spread out. Must have jumped them. Only way.

Then I thought of telling this back home, explaining how the two'n them got shot to death for no reason. Checking up on the bastard was all, I bet, giving him a scare in case he never got the message, as ought to have done since he got done over pretty good, though not like the nigger. He got done over all the way to hell. He were just standing there when we rode in, up there like he was somebody. He'd been fixing to leave. The wagon all loaded with nigger junk. Just not fast enough is all. Telling us it were his place and he'd be obliged. Be obliged? Who the fuck he think he is speaking at us? I thought I seen something over at the woods. Heard he's got a kid. Thought maybe that were it. Then he sees me and starts calling me out. Well, ain't no one going to take that. Me and Tom. Yes, well, Tom was dead, but then he was off his horse and in there grabbing the bastard. Then we strung him up. He didn't say nothing now, not with a rope around his neck.

Inside his place, it was pretty stripped. Moved everything he could, of course. There were some pictures, though, pictures of niggers. We put our boots through a few'n them, then dropped a match or two and let it go. It went all right. We should have done that when he were alive, so he could see it go up. As it was, he was just hanging there with the sparks around him. We got on out but I gave him one for luck. Now Mikey and Tom were out on the grass. All because of that nigger. Shows we should kill 'em all. What in God's name use is they?

It choked me up to see them there and I thought to burn this place, too, but better be on my way. Kill the bastard done it, bring him back here, maybe. Kill him here like he done with them. Fuckin' birds singing like this never happened. Fuckin' birds.

Took them back to Ma and Pa and got the other boys, but it was late by now and getting dark, and though the dogs could track at night, we figured to wait for first light. They weren't going nowhere because there was nowhere as we could figure they could go. Time to bury the boys later, we told ourselves, so we put them in the barn, Pa staying with them to keep the rats off, Ma getting things ready inside. Wants them inside, she says, acting crazy, crying and screaming that did no good. We were going to get the bastards done it, I said. But we were going to get them when we was fresh and they was ruined from running. We were up by four.

Broke out the guns and the rest of the dogs and were off before the light come through. Twenty minutes we were at his place and watching the dogs work back and forward till they found a trail. Then they was off, us following. They went where I reckoned they would, heading for the water. I'd have done the same. We lost them at the stream but any fool could tell where they was heading. Didn't need the dogs, who went all crazy, running back and forth, jumping over it, looking to pick up the trail when there wasn't one. Wasn't one because anyone would know to walk in the water and stay there. John said they maybe gone up the stream, but it were just something to say. We all knew where they heading, so off we go. They on foot, on foot and walking in the stream. We gaining on them every moment. Ain't so easy to go walking through water. Then I realize I'm thinking 'they'. And who the fuck could this 'they' be? Him we knew. And you could see in a way why he done what he done. But who in hell going to be with him? But there must've been two, as it seems to me. No one going to take down Tom and Mikey on his own.

Then we reached the river and this time it weren't so clear. They would stick to the water for a while, for far enough so they would think theirselves clear. This time, though, they might have gone upstream. That's what John thought, saying they would reckon on downstream and how we should go the other way. Could be, I thought, but if it were me I'd have headed on down. Wading against the current would wear you down and we'd broken him up good. Still, he bet that that were the way, so he took two'n the dogs and went off with Jake, needing to split across the river and cover two banks. I went down with Ralph. We got the one dog.

First thing was for one of us to get across to the other side, cover them splitting that way. I can't swim, so he took off, wading, with the dog behind him. After a while, he let go and struck out for the other side, which was why it couldn't be me. The dog was swept further down. It took him time to get out of the middle where the water was fastest. But after a while they both made it and pulled theirselves out. Blackie shook hisself and there was a whirl of spray with a rainbow in it. I seen the rainbow. That mean the fire next time and fire was coming to those we was tracking.

I didn't have no dog so I was going to have to keep close to the water to spot where they stepped out. It were muddy there and it were pretty sure I would catch sight when they did. It slowed me down, though. There was no path here and I had to thread in and out the trees, always checking to see if they had stepped out yet. Then I began to wonder whether they had maybe just drifted down. If they could swim, likely they wouldn't bother with wading. They did that, they'd be getting further away all the time, unless they'd crossed over, in which case Jakey would pick them up and let off a shot.

The trees got closer and it were hard to see the bank. The storm had left things pretty muddy, right enough, but there were places there were rocks and they could have stepped right on out and I wouldn't have found them. The dogs would've but I didn't have the dogs. So I got to thinking. If they had chosen to go downriver, as I thought, why would they have done that? Where was they heading? Then I got to thinking about the train. If'n I were them, I would be heading out as fast as I could, what with half the county heading after them, as they would once Pa got word about. And the more I thought on that, the more likely it seemed. So I figured I'd give up keeping to the river and strike away from it. Circle round and come back to it later. I took the chance they would double back, but why would they do that, seeing that that would bring them straight into anyone who followed? Then I headed back.

I could still hear the dog on the other side of the river. But it weren't the sound he would make if he had found what he was looking for, so I kept on going. I come to the path at last, but after a bit it narrowed right on down and I realized how I would have to leave the mule behind. That was fine with me. Been leading it half the way. Weren't no use to me no more. The further I went, the more I figured as I had got it right. Who was going to stay in the county, and how would anyone get out without no mule or nothing to carry them? It made good sense. So I left her to find her own way back and struck on out. I'd got my rifle and bullets enough for anything I would need, and I wouldn't need much, I reckoned. Seemed like all they had got was a shotgun, and I could stand off a way and just take them down. I got to running, bending low against the branches cutting me. The ground was soft and seemed to spring up as I run. The river wanders all over through there, as if it ain't too anxious to get nowhere, and so it don't. No matter how fast the water run, I reckon you could keep up with it easy if'n you could only cut right through where the trees was. Even so, I reckoned I was outpacing it. And they can't have had too much of a lead.

And what do you take to that man? Last time, he weren't so keen to take us on. I got the rope out half of a mind to do to him what we did for the nigger he stood up for, but I could see how branding him like a steer was a good idea as well. Except if I had gone right on and done it, then two of my brothers would be alive and I wouldn't be sweating like a hog running after him.

He looked pretty scared, too. Said he hadn't done nothing and the nigger hadn't done nothing neither. He won't be doing nothing now, sure enough, I said, and I could see how it were news to him and he shut right on up.

I sure as hell wouldn't reckon to have that car brace on me. It were white-hot and the blue smoke from where we put it to him made your nose wrinkle. Then we was stopped by the car. Didn't turn out to be nothing, neither. Just some kid, I reckon, who wouldn't have given a shit. And if it had've been the sheriff, what that matter? Doing his work for him. Where was he when that nigger went in there? Not that I give a shit for them two. They done us down enough, I reckon. And you ask me now, I'd say that nigger never touched her. I seen him and there's them as would do that and them who wouldn't and I reckon he was one that wouldn't. She'd like him to, though, you bet. Don't suppose anyone else would, including that shrivelled runt who's jewed us out of enough money, you bet. I went to the city once and you could buy stuff there more than ten cents on the dollar cheaper. And when you come to think on it, why should a nigger have wanted her? Even they got some sense of pride, I guess. Still that ain't the point and we weren't wrong about that other one, white on the outside and black on the in. Why else he kill Tom and Mikey for?

I slowed down now. Didn't seem no point in sweating myself up. I could get to the railroad long before them, swing by the river even, see if I could spot them at all. And why had Tom and Mikey gone there? They didn't say nothing to none of us. Figured they'd have fun on their own, I guess. And how come they let him get that close, him with a shotgun and them with rifles? Then I seed it. They was looking at one of them, didn't have no gun, and the other crept up on them from behind and let them have both barrels. Took them both down and had time to reload. They weren't going in there against someone with a shotgun they could see and them with two rifles. So that was it. One shot in the back, the other swinging round in time to get it in the front. Then he reloads, walks up to him and puts another round into him, already on the ground. Fuck him, fuck him. Well, not long now and he'd be getting his.

Then I'm out in the open suddenly and the river's ahead. I've circled round and come back on it. The question is, am I ahead of them or behind? In the distance, I hear the dog, but it's a long way off and what with the river swinging round the way it does, it could be a mile or two if you measured by the river itself. Then I see something move at the edge of the trees and the two of them step right on out where I could see them. It were him all right. But what surprised me more than that was who he with. It were a nigger. When we wrote that on him, I never knew it were real, but here he was with this nigger boy beside him.

I swung the rifle right on up. God knows why they hadn't seen me there. I was right on the edge of the trees, but anyone with sense would have watched out better than them, stepping out into the open the way they done. I squeezed one off and it took him all right. He went on back until I thought he would go in the river, but he straightened up, so I squeezed another. It seemed to me I saw the nigger boy look in my direction, but I squeezed it off. I couldn't see whether I had hit him or not, but it seemed to me I had, because he went right on over into the river, the nigger boy with him. They went in and were swept away. I ran straight on down to see if I could get another shot off, maybe get the nigger kid, but by the time I got there, the river had taken them, swallowed them up. No way they could get out of that, I figured. I felt good. 'Hot damn!' I shouted. 'Hot damn!' Shot him right in the chest, it seemed to me. Then I thought on the nigger and how I'd had no time to get him. But the river was fierce and it didn't seem likely he could climb out. I don't even know as how niggers can swim, leastways not in no river.

I thought to fire a shot to tell my brother, but then realized he would have to be deaf not to hear the first two. Now the question was whether to push on forward, where there was a path, or wait for him so we could follow both sides. Even if he weren't dead when he went in, it were pretty clear to me then that he would be after a bit. The river moves pretty fast here, bouncing off rocks and all, and I had seen where I had hit him. Maybe the nigger might get free, but who ever heard of a nigger swimming in a river like that? I had seen them jumping in a pond, but hell, that weren't like this. He was dead for sure. The both of them. They got Tom and Mikey, but I sure got them. I decided to wait up a bit. I could hear the dog and it was a deal closer now. With him on one side and me on the other, we had got them dead all right, if they weren't dead already. I wanted the bodies, though. Get me the ears to nail on the barn.

After I waited a while, though, and he still didn't come, I figured I had best be on my way. It must have been further than I thought following along the river bank and perhaps there was no way he could cut across on his side. So I took off along the path, running again and looking out to see if he had been washed up somewhere. The river swung out again and I figured to cut across and save the distance, take a chance on him coming to land. The man was dead for sure but the boy maybe might get out.

It turned out a mistake. The trees got pretty close together and I got turned around a deal, which is how come it was several hours before I found myself at the river below the railroad. There was no way to tell where they was but if they had either one of them got out of that river, this was where I would figure they would make for.

I heard the sound of a train whistle in the distance and got a strange feeling. It seemed the smart place for me wasn't down there toward the river but up above, where I could see the bridge reach out above it like a line someone had drawn in the sky. So I started in to climbing, putting the rifle on safety, there being those who had shot theirselves for not doing such. I got up to the top just as she pulled around the corner.

I seen the men working on the engine and then the wagons were going past, not so fast that I couldn't have stepped aboard if I had a mind. I could see nothing of them, but I squatted down to look and, as I did, it seemed to me I could see someone on the other side, running along, only the passing wheels made it difficult to see. And suddenly I knew how it was them but I couldn't get at them because they was on the other side. I slipped the safety and thought to maybe shoot through but saw how that would just hit the wheels. So I ran along to find a place where the wagons were joined and I could get a clear shot. But I had spotted them too late.

Then it was past and I jumped across the rails and pulled the rifle up, squinting along the bridge where it was going. And I think I saw something further along but then it was gone as soon as I saw it and all I could do was watch the caboose, with its red lights, even though it was day, swinging away around the corner and dropping down the hill.

~

He was asleep. The rhythmic de-dum de-dum, de-dum de-dum had rocked him into a half-dream. With part of his mind, he knew where he was, the countryside drawn away behind him like dust settling behind a car, but part was putting fragments of time into a new order. His wife was there, young and laughing, running round the house like she did and him after her, hot and eager, but so was a man with a gun, swinging round slowly to look him in the eye, the laughter there still. Then he was in a river, with no time in between, as if the river had been there all along. His mind was shaking itself gently, getting it all into some kind of pattern. He opened his eyes but didn't exactly wake up. The air was warm and washed over him. There was a pain waiting for him, and he slipped away from it again, so tired that the tiredness was almost a barrier.

He was drifting somewhere, back in the river and the trees above. The sun was on his face and he was in the middle of a sparkle of light. And everything was fine, everything was just as it should be. And he could hear the wash of water and laughter that had the sound of water rushing over rocks.

Then he was jolted back into wakefulness. The engineer had pulled on the brakes so that a chain of clangs passed the length of the train, like a message, if he could only have understood what it said. Then it was picking up speed again, but the noise had woken him and he opened his eyes, feeling the ache in his shoulder as he did so.

For the first time, as it seemed to him, he had time to think. He was pulling away from danger. Each double clack of the wheels put him further from those who wished him dead. But he knew, too, that he had no idea where he might be going. Get away from the boy. A voice inside told him he must get away from the boy. What good to stick together now, when they were away from those who knew what had happened? The thing was to strike out in different ways. He guessed the boy must have some place to go. Then again, just because he didn't know where he was didn't mean that others wouldn't. He turned to the boy but he was asleep, mouth open, lying like a puppy by the fire. And he was a boy. He could no more fix an age to him now than he had before. But there was more to him than you would think. And he had saved him twice, for he remembered, now, the body that thudded into him, took him forwards and into the river when he had taken one bullet and might have been expected to take another. The train clanged again as the brakes bit hard and this time it was the boy who woke, staring straight up at the roof, looking puzzled, before recalling where he was, it seemed, since he turned towards him now and looked him in the eye.

'How you doing?'

There was no reply, as how could there be when the boy was dumb? Been with him so long, he had put it out of mind, no longer asking himself how it could be so, accepting now that he would stay as closed in as he was.

'You take a look at my shoulder?'

The boy sat up. He looked worn out. Doubtless they both looked worn out, considering what had happened to them and where they had been. He got up just the same, making his way toward him while balancing against the movement, black, his clothes torn through and a glisten of red blood against the black where a rock or a branch had opened him up. He sat down beside him, close to where the open door gave them a view of what was passing. And what was passing was mostly trees and fields as it had been since they had climbed on board, however long ago that had been. The boy reached out but he could see there was nothing he could do unless he took his shirt off. So he leaned away and eased himself out of it, though that wasn't as easy as it seemed and he had to let the boy help, pulling one arm out and then swinging it around back before peeling it down the other. He was gentle enough, bracing himself as the train rocked back and forth and lurched, occasionally, as if the wagon were catching up with the one in front and then letting it go again.

He glanced down at his shoulder. It was red around the wound but it was clean enough, dark at the centre where the bullet went in, and puckered some, but clean. He looked down at his chest and though it was the mess he expected it to be, he could see that even so soon the skin was beginning to form, though it was tight and painful where the letter had been burnt. He held his hand out in front, the hand that he'd used to push the car brace away, and he noticed that he could open it further now. The burn was still there, clear enough, white crusted with black, but the time in the water seemed to have softened it some. In fact, it seemed to him that he had emerged from that baptism a great deal better than he had gone in.

There was nothing for the boy to do. They didn't have anything to put on, except he remembered the jar of cream he had slipped in his inside pocket. He put his hand in. He thought it might have broken. It would hardly be surprising if it had, but it was still there. Some of the cream was there, too. Mostly it was a smear around the sides but there was some at the bottom so that he could hook his finger in and bring a clot out. He spread it on his chest, leaving the hand to heal itself. There were bits of fluff in among it but there was just enough to outline the letter, soften the hard-edged scab, lift some of the pain away.

The boy watched him do it, watched as the letter was spelled out in white. Then he shrugged and went back to where he had been sitting before, staring between his legs when he slumped down, staring as if he were trying to figure out where they were going to and why he was here, as why would he not whose life had been turned around as much as it had been, no more having a map to follow than did the man he found himself with.

Outside, the land rose as a series of hills swung into view, hills with still others behind them, green edging to purple. The engine began to labour, the wagons to clang against one another so that the man had to reach out a hand and steady himself. It was strange, this feeling of being drawn along in a direction not of his choice, this sense that he had surrendered his fate not to another man but to this machine, straining against the land, cutting through it as if it could go wherever it wished. Somehow his mind was still back there in the only place he knew. He was unused to floating free, being carried into the future. Where he came from, he knew the past. Every stain on his table, every crevice in the wall, every broken fence post, every rock and gulley had a past, prompted a memory, told him that he belonged. Now he was where hills lifted into the sky and there were places and people as strange to him as he would be to them. And yet the train was his protection. As long as he stayed on the train, that future would never become anything as definite as a place. He had nothing to explain and nobody to explain it to.

The hills were giving way to what could only be called mountains, at least to one who had never seen such, never seen hills that went beyond a certain height, the kind of height that hills were meant to be. They edged up into a sky that went from blue to turquoise to white. There were clouds gathered around the top of them as though it were the mountains themselves that made them. The rest of the sky was that relentless blue that could bear down on you and, though the train made a wind of its own, the air itself was still thick and sweaty, though thinning now, cooling a little. He sat with his back to the edge of the door, knees drawn up, watching as trees came toward him so that he could reach out a hand and take a leaf. He closed his eyes, not content, running as he was, even here on the train, running from, running toward, but at rest for a second as if at last it had relented, the whole thing, one thing after another, until his head had spun and his body had done what it had to do, not knowing why, except what else was there to do? Fifty-one years old, he thought, and shook his head without knowing he did so. Fifty-one years old.

The wagon was empty, except for what looked like a pile of rags in the far corner. None the less, there was a smell that he couldn't quite track down. It wasn't there when he first climbed in, or if it was, it was lost in the rush and the fear. It was a mixture of sweet and sour and it hung on the air like the smell of verbena, though not verbena, something else, something he knew nothing of but that recalled a smell he knew. And even the breeze which spun wisps of straw on the floor of the wagon, and lifted his hair which before had been slicked to his forehead, even that didn't clear it away. And then he began to wonder what it might be, remembering, suddenly, a rat trapped under the stoop that had rotted one summer and filled the air with flies. And as he remembered, so he looked around and where could it come from but from the pile of rags? After a while, he made his way to it and stirred it, standing up, finding his balance, and walking splay-legged so as not to fall. He stirred it with his feet. Then he stopped and crouched down. He lifted a piece of sacking and then stopped, sucking in his cheeks, shaking his head, as the wagon rocked from side to side and the bright countryside slid away behind. There was a touch of doom about him, right enough. No matter how hard he tried to get away, it was chasing right on after him. The boy must have detected something as well, because he came across and crouched down beside him and they both stared into the dead eye of the old man, the other missing, plucked out as if a raven had come in and flown off with it to its nest, dead men's eyes gathered like eggs to be hatched into monsters.

The bitter smell was from where he had pissed and voided himself. The sweet was from where he seemed to be rotting away. The man reached a hand out but then withdrew it.

'Can't have been dead long, just the same. How far the train come? Can't have been dead that long.'

Even so, there was a smell and strong enough that he wondered why they hadn't noticed it before or, if noticing it, and he realized that he had, why they hadn't tried to find out what it might be.

'This has maybe come up from the Gulf. Then again, perhaps it just sat in a siding. Wouldn't take much to turn him, not in this heat.'

What he really wanted to know was why he was dead. Had he just given out, riding the rails to God knows where, or was there something else besides? He lifted a torn jacket that might have once been worth something, though a long time ago. And as he lifted it, he saw there was blood down his front, black and red and drying to powder. It didn't make sense, his having blood there, except that he was soaked with it, had bathed in it, as it seemed. And to the right, where his heart was, the man facing him but seeing nothing, with one eye gone and the other dead, was a tear in his shirt and another beside it, and another, too.

'God,' he said. 'He been killed. And don't we look like just the folks as would have done it, with nothing to show for ourselves and me all shot to hell? We gotta get out of here, kid. We gotta get off this train before they find us with him. They'd just as soon hang us for this as for anything else they have in mind. We gotta jump.'

As if to frustrate the thought, at that very moment the train began to pick up speed, deciding, finally, it seemed, where it was off to and wanting to get there fast. The land must have levelled out, though he had thought it was no more than a series of hills, mountains, rising up by steps as far as he could see. He peered at the man, but if he had a secret, he didn't offer it up. He could see by the cut in his red shirt that he had been knifed, and since people don't knife themselves, and even if they did, would hardly be likely to take the knife out and throw it away, some-one had obliged him before going off. 'First time it slows, we off. It don't matter how far we come or where we are.'

But how far had they come? He was far from sure how long

they had been on board and knew nothing of where the train went, except to the north. But even he knew that the north was an idea and not a place. Then the engineer put his brakes back on and they both fell down, the pain shooting through him, separating himself from himself as a knife would do, as a knife had done for the one who slid to the side now and down on to his face, staring out of the door through his one good, dead eye.

He was on his feet again immediately and edging to the door.

'Come on, boy. This is as far as we go.'

He put his head out of the doorway and then pulled it back in again. He had seen a depot coming towards them, a water tank looming up like some animal, an elephant, he guessed, with its trunk hanging down.

'Quick, we arriving somewhere. Gotta jump before they sees us.'

And, not waiting for the boy, he leaned out, hesitated a second and jumped. He landed on both feet and tried to stagger forwards, to break into a run and keep pace with the train, but his feet had gone from under him and he was falling forwards and then rolling sideways down an incline. Each time he turned over, he felt the pain of his wounds. The train sounded its whistle and covered a scream he let out without his even knowing that he had. He came to rest near a bunch of nettles, curious glad that he hadn't stung himself, curious because every nerve was screaming back at him from where he had scraped and torn himself in the fall. He lay for a second, his head spinning, half-expecting someone to call out, half-expecting a bullet, since there always seemed to be someone waiting to shoot him down. When at last he did sit up, there was the boy, holding his arm and sobbing silently. It was bust. It didn't take a doctor to see that. Only it wasn't. He saw now that it was out of its socket, sticking out in an odd way as if it didn't belong to him but had just been stuck on. Suddenly he was glad that the boy was dumb, though he was making a noise, a kind of strangled cry covered by the whistle which blew again to announce its arrival.

'Here, boy,' he said. 'You popped your arm. For God's sake, keep quiet. I can get it straight for you.'

And he could, having done so before, being taught when his father put his back in when he fell from the roof when he had been wanting to fly, learning that he couldn't, learning, too, that things were never as you thought they might be. He came round in front of the boy and put one hand gently against his shoulder. With the other, he took hold of his wrist.

'Just look in my eyes, boy. Don't look nowhere else. This'll hurt for a moment and I wouldn't tell you other. But it'll be over fast. Listen,' he said, 'that a woodpecker?'

The boy half-turned his head and he pushed hard on the shoulder and twisted the wrist. There was a sucking noise and a popping sound and the arm eased straight on back into place. The boy looked down at his arm as if he had lost it and someone had just come up and given it back. He nodded.

'Ain't nothing,' said the man, oddly pleased that he had been able to do something in return for the boy saving him not once but twice. 'Let's get going. Just get away from here and think a piece.'

There was a pine wood across an open field, but a ditch ran along the side of the field, so they could reach the trees without being seen, unless someone chose to stand on top of the water tower which they could see behind them as they crouched low and ran. It was hot now they were off the train. The breeze had kept things cool, but out here there was no wind at all and the sun beat down, though it must have been late in the day, judging where it was. It took them no more than fifteen minutes before they were in among the trees, the earth red and brittle as if it hadn't seen rain in an age. They sat down then, him with his back against the wood, the boy half-lying, looking toward the station, where they could see the train standing while water gushed down into the engine. Someone was walking back down the train, checking the wagons. Whoever it was was getting close to where they had been, close to where a man's dead body was who had been killed by someone else, someone long gone, leaving them to gather up the blame. And if that person walking along the track, checking each wagon as he passed it, found that man, then everything would change. But someone called him from the front. They could hear the sound across the fields and in the shade of the trees, and the man made his way back to the engine where two other men were standing, moving slowly enough, as if nothing mattered enough to pick up speed, as out here why would it, there being nothing around, nothing but an engine taking on water and a bunch of men just standing there.

They stood for a while, then one of them reached up and swung the soft tube that had been gushing water away from the engine, still flooding silver. It dribbled to a halt, like a man taking a pee, getting done and turning away. Two men climbed back into the engine while the other walked back to the shed that was all there was to the depot. The whistle sounded and the wheels spun for a second till they got a grip and then with a series of metal bangs and clangs, running back through the train, it began to pull away, moving slow against the gradient, jumping itself forward with shunts from behind where the wagons seemed to want to go faster than the engine calculated possible.

Behind them, the hills rose up away from the track. He had

no idea where he was. Ten minutes before and he had been content that they were edging ever further from the consequences of their actions, moving toward something unknown but redemptive. Ten minutes ago and he had known that when at last he did get down from the train, he and the boy would go in different directions since it was them being together that was the root of the problem. Separate, they could become invisible. Who would notice a white man among his own or a black boy with his? But here together they were chained as much as if they had been convicts like those he used to see strung beside the highways, sweating in the sun, unable to lift a hand without it pulled on the one beside him. Well, that was the way they were again. How could they separate when he had no idea where they were and had had evidence enough that he needed someone along, that he would have been dead twice over if the boy hadn't been along, even if the boy or his father was who had caused him the trouble? And where would the boy be without him who but a moment before had been doubled in pain with an arm that was useless, just waiting for them to seek him out? No, he knew that whatever they did they would do together until things settled somewhat, until he could think his way through this, though his mind was as confused as it had ever been.

'Best get away from the line,' was all he could think and all he could say and the boy saw the sense of it, getting up straight away and flexing his arm to see it was still working, still in its place.

He looked up through the trees, but there was nothing to see but the land rising up. Then it came to him that that was perhaps what they needed: to get up high where they could see all around, where they could see the lie of the land, spot those who might follow, understand where they might be and see where they could go. Before, he had thought that maybe it was a town they needed. People got lost in towns. No one knew anyone there, he had been told. All were strangers. But where was a town? And besides, he could never get by in such a place, would never know what to do. The land he knew. And so did the boy who had caught him a rabbit with nothing more than a rock, as it seemed. Well, they could do better than that together. And they were free. For the moment, that was what mattered most. To be free. There were two men dead and now another that might be put down to them, though they knew nothing of him, nothing of what had happened and who might have done it.

'We'd best climb up a piece.'

And so they set off, the air freshening a little, as it seemed to him, though it was hot enough still, the sweat smarting on his neck and burning his chest and his shoulder. And as he climbed, the pain reminded him that his body could go bad. He knew to keep the wounds clean, but how was that to be done, rolling in the dirt, sweating like this? He would need to look for water, need the boy to check on him. It didn't pay, maybe, to be alone. First thing was to get better, to heal a bit. Maybe, he thought, they could find a place to hole up, let his body get back into shape. Maybe then he would be able to think straight, as at the moment he was none too sure that he could.

$\sim$

The train went right off and there were nothing I could do. They were on it for sure. I seen their legs under it. I started running, got halfway across before I saw it weren't no good. I stood looking every way, not knowing which to take. Quickest way back was along the track to the station. Take maybe a couple'n hours. But what would I need to go there for? I could call the sheriff, round up some people, but this was family. No cause to bring others in. If I did, though, they could call ahead, get it stopped so we could catch up. But once the sheriff were on to this, we would never get at them at all. Worst would be that some other sheriff got in on it, too, put them in jail some other place, let them get off, let them get away. No, I weren't going for that. But how could I get the others? One brother over the river somewhere, the others off in the wrong direction. It wouldn't take Ralphy no time to get here, but there was no crossing the river. He would have to get back where he crossed first time.

The others would know by now that they was heading the wrong way, but then what would they do? Would they come on this way or maybe go back? And if they came this way, which side of the river would they go? The more I thought, the less I knew what to do and all the time the nigger and his friend was getting away, going north where maybe we wouldn't get to reach them, shoot 'em down. At last I decided the best thing would be to track back. I could call across the river and then get to meet the others. Best thing then would be to get a truck and run up the road, close as we could get to the railroad. I started out, running at first and then walking, figuring that running wouldn't count in the end. Then I got to thinking. How would we know where they got off? They jump on, they could jump off anywhere. Fair bet they would stay on long as they thought we might be there, but what then? And how fast would it go? It would be two hours or more before we could set off and how fast does a train go? I never been on no train nor never wanted to. Why would I want that, going off somewhere? But how fast do they go? Maybe they went right on up north. I started in to running again and then saw my brother across the water.

'They jumped the train,' I shouted.

The dog turned around him, all excited.

'What?' he called back, the noise of the water making it difficult to hear.

'The nigger and him jumped a train up by the bridge.'

'What nigger?' he asks.

'The kid.'

He shrugs his shoulder, not knowing about the nigger.

'You see him?' he shouted.

'Of course I seen him. How else would I know?'

'What you doing, going that way?'

'Got to go back, get the truck. Get the others, too. You keep on over there, case the others crossed. Go back and we'll meet at the house.'

'You reckon we can catch him?'

'Course we catch them. They ain't getting away.'

'Cause he killed two'n ours.'

'I know they killed two'n ours.'

He were never bright. Got kicked in the head when he were four and never been the same. Even so, he weren't simple.

'I'm going,' I said.

'Right,' he shouted. 'Where are you going?'

'Back,' I said. 'I told you before.'

'Right,' he shouted, and even then I wasn't so sure he knew what was happening.

I found his gun. I was crossing the open where I shot him and there was his shotgun, shining in the sun. I still couldn't see how he got out of the river, let alone climbs on a train, running along as I see him do. Or at least his legs. I seen his legs. Then I thought that maybe it wasn't him. I only seen their legs. But who else would be jumping a train? And what white man would be with a nigger, besides? I picked up the shotgun. It were too good for him. At least I got something to show, I thought. Then I thought how when I caught up with him I'd shoot him in the head with it. That seemed the right thing to do. Pay back. I broke it open but there weren't no shells in it. I guess he was out of ammunition.

It took me best part of couple hours before I run into the rest. They'd been wasting their time backtracking up the stream when it was obvious he wouldn't have gone that way. You could jump over it some places and where would they have been heading for if they had gone that way? I told them what I had seen and we decided on home. Just then there was a splashing and the dog come over the river. He'd run ahead of my brother.

'We going for the sheriff?' he called as he crossed over behind it.

'Shit the sheriff. This ain't his business. It ours. Let's get us back and head on out.' Which is what we did, only we took time to get us something to eat and decide to take a fresh dog. Just the one. We didn't see as how there'd be much tracking to do. Just find where they got to, if'n they did, seeing that I never seed them, not really, so as you could say. We filled the tank from the cans kept out back. It were a crap truck but it would do for what we needed, just driving up the state road that run right close to the railroad for a good bit. Seemed like we should be able to catch up in good time. Pa said it had to stop and take on water and if it were a freight they often laid up a piece to load this and that. He asked about the sheriff, too, which seemed pretty strange to me. I thought he would be the one who said to keep it in the family. But the sheriff had come, as if he knew we'd be talking about him.

~

He turned off the ignition and let it come to a halt on its own. This was as far as he could get without risk of scraping it on branches or running over a rock. It was his car and not the department's and with only a hundred and fifty on the clock he was damned if he was going to take any chances. He sat there a while, tapped a cigarette out and lit it. He didn't flip the match out of the window. There were those that did and it took days to get the fire out. He picked a piece of tobacco off his tongue and looked at himself in the mirror. The hair was receding. Well, it would, stuck in a place where nothing happened and when it did you would as soon be somewhere else. But you took work where it was. Pity his wife hadn't understood as much. All the windows were wound down. You could bake in weather like this, not that there was any other kind around here. Which was maybe why they were like they were. You couldn't call it police work. The odd still or two and a dozen jugs buried out back. Things went on inside some of these places you didn't want to think about. They were even illegal, but who wanted to get into that. Brothers and sisters and who knows what else. And now this race thing. It seemed they could live without it a year or two and then something boils up in their blood, some cancer starts growing and they got to cut it out, no matter what.

His job was not to know about it until later. Not too difficult at that. No one was going to tell him until it was over and by then there was nothing to do but call in the coroner or more likely the mortician since there wasn't much point in stirring things up. This was the place he was and this was how this place was. If he had known, he'd have stopped it. He wasn't like them. The day he became like them was the day he would take off for anywhere and never mind if there were jobs to go to. He would have stopped it and they would have gone along with it. Sure, they would have hated him at the time, spoiling their fun and all, but when they sobered up and it went out of their blood, they would have seen the point. Or if they didn't, and perhaps they wouldn't, they would leave it at that since leaving things as they were was their special talent, which was how things got to be as they were. Crap.

He picked another piece of tobacco off his tongue and was tapping a cigarette out of the pack before he thought what he was doing, stopping himself at the last moment from lighting it from the other. That was what his days had been mostly about for a long time now, coffee on tasteless coffee, cigarette on tasteless cigarette. The filters were to stop him from dying. All they did was stop him from tasting. He lit it, not noticing he was doing so, and then, noticing, stubbed it out in the tray before thinking better of it. It was a new car and he liked to keep it clean. He swept it out with his finger, cupping his hand beneath it and then throwing it away. It had taken all his savings, but what were savings for, now she had up and left, now there were no plans worth the planning for? He stared ahead through the woods, wondering whether there was any point to this. He had already been to where they had strung the black man up, a man he had seen around and who never caused any trouble that he knew, except that he was his own man and around here that wasn't supposed to be. He had thought he would find him still swinging there, but instead found nothing but ashes. Even thought they had burnt him up in there, that he had got his information wrong, because if there was one thing they liked more than a rope, it was flames. But then he found the grave, a spade standing upright as if someone had meant it for a cross, and since there was no way that any of those that had done that would have thought to bury him this way, there had to be someone else. And his bet was the boy. There was a young kid, maybe fourteen or some, used to come in with him on the cart. Bright enough. That was who must have done it, him or some other black man drifting out of nowhere and going back as fast. Still, his bet was on the boy.

But did that mean he saw it? He knew what had happened, or thought he did. There were those that were happy to tell him when once it was done and there was nothing he could do to stop anything. They didn't make a mention of a boy. And since the one they lynched, and that was the word, was buried so neat, he had to know that they had not caught up with him, at least not then, though they were thorough enough when they tried. Didn't like to leave stones unturned, people alive who could be dead. No, he must have hid and then come out later, and if he had any sense at all, if he was as bright as he seemed when he and his father came into town, then he would have left out of here long since and been on his way to somewhere else, anywhere else at all.

Then there was the other, the other that had brought him up here, where he seldom came, having no reason to except when he went hunting sometimes, squeezing off at whatever moved as if it was the people he ought to have been shooting but couldn't. They had told him about this other, too. Gone directly on to him after they done hanging and burning the other, meaning, no doubt, to do much the same, only not doing so in the end, at least as he was told, but knocking him around some. There was talk of some fire, too, of marking him 'so folks would know'. And which folks were these, he had to ask? Everyone here knew everything. Even him, though it was often a day or two before word got through. Odd thing was that they knew he would have to do something if he knew for sure, but once it was done, who would he get to swear to it? They would let him know, at least the one or two he had a lean on would, or those who couldn't hold it in, wanting to hear themselves talk about something as if doing it weren't enough and it was necessary to hear it over again even if it was their own voices they heard.

So he was here to check it out, see how bad hurt he was, see whether he wanted to bring charges, as would be a fool to do so since there were guns enough hereabouts to equip a division or two and then some. But he had to check. He found himself lighting another cigarette, as though he had no mind of his own and no will either. He rubbed it out in the ashtray and then blew so that the dust flew up. He brushed at his clothes and put the cigarette back in the pack, noting that there were fewer than he had expected. He opened the door and stepped outside. The heat was what it ever was and there was a dank smell, rich and loamy. A bird whirred through the trees, a flash of red. He felt better out here, better than in town where there was no way of getting away from the heat and nothing to look at but the road or the railroad tracks and nothing to look forward to except the next cup of coffee or the next cigarette.

He ran his hands along the shiny black paint of the Ford. There was something real about that, real enough to take all his savings. He took a deep breath. There was something sweet in the air, some flower he couldn't see but was blooming there in the soft light for no purpose but to seed another. No different from us, he thought, and struck a match, holding it for a second before realizing there was no cigarette to be lit. Bad, he thought, bad. He set off up the track. It was no more than half a mile further and there were worse things to be doing. What would he say when he got there? What was there to say? But it was his job to say it. Whatever it was. It would be easy enough when he started. But he would get nothing back. These people weren't talking people. They mostly worked like dogs and drank like pigs and slept in the sun and that was about it. Every now and then they would pull a knife or shoot off a gun, and then he would take them in, but mostly they would just live from day to day, if you could call what they did living, if you could call what he did living.

When he stepped into the clearing, nothing moved. He stood still for a second, taking it in. The shack was like a dozen others, hid away here, falling down, as it seemed to him, and placed where nobody would want to come. There would be a well and an outhouse and that would about do it. No real-estate man would ever come by. These places were never sold. If someone died or, less likely, moved on, they would simply leave it and either someone else of a like mind would come on by, maybe some relative living in worse, if you could imagine worse, or it would rot away until the woods took it and the clearing back again as if it had all been a mistake. And who was to say it hadn't been?

Yet he could see how someone might take a liking to this place. There was nowhere else hereabouts that you could say was so much better and at least here you were on your own, as this man was. He hardly knew him, to tell the truth, but he had asked around. Seems there had been a wife once, and even a kid for an hour or two, but that was long ago and he had been content since to be alone. Doubtless, like the other men, he would cat around a little, go to those towns nearby that catered for such as him. Well, from what he heard he wouldn't be doing that for a while.

He had thought to bring the doctor out but figured it was better to check things first. Billy had only seen things through the woods, out with his girl in the family car. It was that car that had made him want one himself. There was money in death, his father being a mortician. Anyway, Billy, being out with a girl, hadn't wanted people to know who told the sheriff and wouldn't have gone that way if he had known, looking to do his business with Linda Sue who, if he did but know it, had done her business with most of the town.

He stepped out into the light, noticing, as he did, that the door was stood wide. He looked around, half-expecting to see him standing there. People left doors open here. They were honest in some things and crooks and perverts and psychotics and simply dumb in others. 'Can't be that bad,' he thought to himself, 'not if he's out and about.' He slowed a little. It never paid to walk straight on into anywhere when you didn't know what might be waiting for you the other side. He could hear nothing, besides the birds and crickets. No one chopping wood or singing to himself, not that he would have been doing that if it was true.

He stopped by the door and then reached in and knocked. There was no reply. He knocked again, sure, now, that there was no one in. Then he stepped inside. Everything looked as you might expect. Nothing worth spit, in fact almost nothing at all. He stood in the kitchen, looking around. There was a rag in the corner had what looked a lot like blood. So there was something in it right enough. He stepped through into the bedroom and looked at the bed, red-black with blood. So, they had got their man all right, done whatever it was that they wanted done. And he had lain down here. The question was how bad he had been hurt. Then he looked across at where a piano was pushed up against the wall. Not a sight you saw much, and if at all, not in the bedroom, though there was nowhere else it could go, not in this pinched little house. He crossed over and lifted the lid, thick with dust except where someone had run their hand along it, drawing a bright black line. He played a note. It was silent. He tried another. It sounded like a bar-room honky-tonk left to ruin. He closed the lid and looked around. What kind of man would have a piano? Then another thought, right away. Not a man but a woman, of course, a woman long gone so that this was what remained. Not played, but kept. He nodded to himself and went back into the kitchen to give it a closer look.

He saw where there were two cups set out and two bowls beside. This didn't fit with what he had been told. Who was this other person? Who had come to call and looked after him, as it seemed? Then, out of the corner of his eye, he saw the shell cases, lying under a chair, red and gold. Seeing them did something to him. Until then he had been none too interested. He was just checking things out to see they were as he'd been told. He knew nothing would come of it. No one would talk, no one would want him around. But the sight of those shell cases changed things round. He bent down and picked them up. What were they doing there? People didn't shuck cases on to the floor and leave them there. If they were out hunting, they flipped them out where they were. If they came on back, they would put them somewhere. The place was pretty neat, bare but neat, and he couldn't see how the man would have just dropped them down. So what were they doing there? He smelt them, pressing them in turn to his nose. They were recent. The smell was still strong. Then where was the gun? He couldn't recall seeing one. He stepped back into the bedroom, bent down and looked under the bed. There was something under there but it wasn't a gun.

He pulled the bed away from the wall. There were two things. One was a shoebox, its top half off, the other was a piece of floorboard, lifted up. He pulled the bed further into the room. Something scuttled away and he put his hand to his gun, a reflex, nothing more. The floor was thick with dust except where someone had done what he had done and pulled the bed out, because he could see the marks.

He reached inside the space where the floorboard had been, turning his head aside as he reached his hand in, thinking, briefly, of the spider that could put him in hospital or the snake that could end things right there. But what he felt was the cool of a glass jar. He pulled it out. The top was missing, so he reached back inside and found it, bottom side up, lying just inside so that he was surprised he had missed it at first. And what could have been in there that was worth hiding, that you might store in a jar against the moment you might need it? What else but money, no one hereabouts trusting banks, as they were right not to, others having lost money when they went bust, as they did when times were hard, which was when you needed them most.

But why would this man have taken his money from under the floorboards? Why else but that he was on his way, running, knowing that those who cut him or whatever they did might think to finish the job.

He slid the shoebox toward him and ran his fingers through it. Nothing here. Some tissue paper, a piece of cloth and a book, a gospel, and nothing more that anyone would keep, let alone run off with, except that there were spaces where something else had been, one staining a circle on the brown cardboard, a jar of something perhaps. He raised the box and sniffed at it. There was a perfume there. But why would anyone running want to take perfume along with him, unless it reminded him of someone used to wear it maybe? Even then, if I was running, he thought, I wouldn't take anything such along with me, but then I wouldn't want anything reminded me of her. Something else had been there because there was a piece of tissue paper all balled up, but what that was there was no means of saying.

He went back into the kitchen and sat himself down again to think. Here was a man, then, lived all alone, if what they said were true. He got cut up or beaten so bad that he chose to leave where he had lived for all his life. He opened up the floor where he had stored such as he had, carried with him some perfume so he would carry with him a memory that otherwise was part of this place, and then took off. But there was something wrong with that. Two things wrong with that. First, he wasn't alone. There had been someone else, and it wasn't one of those who wanted to hurt him because this person had eaten and drunk with him. And then there were the two shell cases. And while perhaps they were from some other time, left there so he forgot them, it didn't seem likely, what with them smelling as fresh as they did. Now, what story could be made to fit all that?

He looked at the pot, left in the sink unwashed, and smelt that as he had smelt other things, smelling, in his experience, being as good as anything to find things out. It was rabbit, so maybe the shells were from that. But who did the shooting and who would come out here to a man fingered by those others who could do folks harm? Then a thought struck him, a thought so unlikely that he nearly dismissed it out of hand. But a phrase came back to him from what he had been told had happened down at the store, the thing that had justified all that happened afterwards. 'Stood up for a nigger,' he had been told, unlikely as that sounded. But, then, everything he had been told seemed unlikely to him. He knew those that ran the store. They were old and bitter and she was as ugly as sin itself and nobody, but nobody, would ever make a move in her direction unless they had lost all of their wits. None the less, that was what he had been told. So, could it be that the other person who had eaten with him was maybe black, and if black, who else but the person who dug a grave for his father, knowing that they might be back for him, and not knowing, of course, what they had done to this man? But even as he tried the idea out, it seemed impossible. This wasn't a place where black sought out white or white sought out black. They got by never looking to each other for anything.

He got up and stood in the doorway. Then he spun around and went back in. He found what he was looking for almost straight away. A box of shells, only there were no more than half a dozen. And why didn't he take more than that, he asked himself, answering the question by seeing in his mind a man running off in panic, grabbing what he could, abandoning the food left in the pot. He stepped outside again, wondering to himself which direction he might have gone. And as he stared, unseeing, as you might have thought, trying to figure where he would have gone if he had been in the same fix, he saw where the grass had got pushed down and scuffed up no more than a dozen paces away.

He walked across to it, wondering what might have caused it, crouching down finally, noticing right away the blood smeared on the grass. And no more than half a dozen paces further on, he found more of the same and parallel gouges where someone had been dragged a little before being lifted up. So, two people shot. But who the hell were they? Was it the two who had set off to get away but left it too late, or was it some others? And if it was, then who the hell might they be? He walked around the clearing to see if there were any more marks, to see if anyone had maybe dragged the bodies, if bodies there were, off into the scrub. But there was nothing to be seen, nothing he could see.

He went back to the trampled area and sat down beside it, trying to see in his mind what might have happened there. Two people inside, with a shotgun and two shots fired. Not, he now thought, to kill a rabbit, as who would need two blasts from a shotgun to do that and what would be left, assuming that someone had? So, two shots for something else. And were they fired from there? He got up and went back inside the kitchen, turning round and looking out to where he had been. It was possible, he could see, though more likely you would have to step outside. But that would mean that those who did the shooting were those trying to flee, which meant the man, because the boy could never have done that, would not have been trusted with a gun, unless the man was incapable of such.

On the other hand, wasn't it more likely that those doing the shooting would be those who had sought them out? And if they had known there was a nigger there — he caught himself using the word, who would not have used it until he came here to find a place where it was used as you would call a tree a tree — well, then, they would have been doubly sure to shoot him down. Hence the two shell cases. Because maybe there was no shotgun in the house. Maybe the shotgun belonged to those that came this far out to finish the job, discovering that they could finish two jobs at the same time. Except there was a box of shells and it wasn't likely that anyone would have brought such along, and if they had, unlikely they would have left them where he found them. Were they killed inside, then? He looked around, carefully this time, searching every wall, running his fingers over the pictures peeling from the bedroom wall, look-ing everywhere that shotgun pellets might have hit, convincing himself, finally, that whoever had fired had done so outside in that there was no sign it had been in here.

He knew he was missing something. There was a story and he didn't know what it might be. He was going to have to come at this some other way. He flipped another cigarette out of the pack and snapped a match with his fingernail, lighting it as the flare died down.

Now who would be visiting out here, who would be coming looking to maybe kill this man or at least to do him further harm? That was an easy question to answer. There was one family that was behind this as they were behind most things that needed a twisted mind. One thing was sure, it wasn't the storekeeper, who would have been scared to set foot in the woods, who would have been content for someone else to do his business. So that meant he had another visit to make, another place to go before the pieces would maybe come into some kind of pattern.

He flicked his cigarette outside and then thought better of it and walked across and crushed it into the earth, picking it up afterwards and putting it in his pocket. Enough of his training had stayed with him that he was going to be sure to keep the crime scene clean. He set off down the track, thinking to himself that this was better than sitting in a fly-blown office and listening to the fan whirl round, turning slowly so that you only got cool once every thirty seconds or so. He walked, feeling the earth springing beneath his feet, until he saw his Ford sitting there in the shade but with a flash of brightness coming back to him from where a patch of sun made its way through the trees. It made him feel good to have the Ford and it made him feel good to be thinking again, trying to figure out what had happened from what he could find, using his brain again as most of the time he did not.

He drove back to the highway, if you could call it a highway, that crumbled at the edges and had a slope that could pull you into the ditch, did pull many a car and truck into the ditch, especially when its driver was too drunk to care over much where it went. From there, he set out for the one place he could maybe make some sense of all the pieces that were floating around in his head.

They were torturing him, maybe getting ready to do more. That's what he had been told and, even though he hadn't believed it, coming as it did from a young man who had been known to stretch the truth somewhat, he had gone on out and found evidence that someone had at least bled a little, that at least two shots had been fired from a shotgun that wasn't there any more, and that someone or something had been dragged a way before being lifted, and if it was bodies, they didn't appear to have been buried, at least not so far as he could see. Which left ... what? It left the Steadmans, or at least a visit there to see if they would deny everything, which was what they usually did, even when you had got them plumb centre and with evidence dropping out of the sky. But who was dead? Was anybody dead?

There was no sign on the track he took, not least because no one would care to go where he was going unless invited, and even not then, because who would trust an invitation from the Steadmans? Not a girl in the neighbourhood would be seen even talking to them, which raised the question of how they managed to keep on coming, there being no shortage of Steadmans, no shortage at all. He had seen them come into town in a truck that had no business on the road, crawling with Steadmans of every age. Well, it was pretty clear that if no girl would be seen with them, they were generating it all by themselves. Each year a new one would turn up at the school. They would even stay a year or two, as if they were sent there just to keep them out of the way. Then they would leave, not a whit wiser than when they arrived but having corrupted a kid or two so that it took years to get them back on track again. Then, twelve months later would come another one, looking just the same, only sorrier and stupider than the last.

There was a mailbox a hundred yards or so along the track, but they never got any mail, except the summonses that were issued on a regular basis and which they paid no more attention to than they would a man from Mars who thought to land at their place. And if it came to such an encounter, he knew which side he would put his money on. To tell the truth, no one ever went up against the Steadmans and came out on top, or even came out at all, it was thought. Even the sheriff's uniform didn't make much sense to them. The best he had managed was to throw them in jail when they got drunk and smashed things up in the bar that was tolerated on the edge of town, though regularly denounced from the pulpit of the church. But that was how things were thereabouts. This was a dry county if you cared to read the statutes, but nobody was reading them and the Steadmans couldn't if they tried, despite the regulation two years they spent at school, ruining others who might have made something of themselves, or more probably not.

No one knew how many of them there were. There were censuses, of course, when everyone was supposed to tell you about themselves, but no census taker had ever ventured out to see them, more than one form being faked by the man assigned to ask them what they did and with whom and for why.

He swung round the corner and there it was. There wasn't just the one place, but a cluster of buildings no one of which could really be called a house. Most looked as though they were put up for animals, which didn't seem so far from the truth. There were several kids playing in the mud and though here he was, driving a brand new Ford, not one of them looked up to see who this might be. He banged his horn in irritation and a mule wandered out in front of him, as though seeing a chance for suicide that would relieve him of the suffering that was doubtless his lot. He stopped and a swirl of dust temporarily shrouded him. He waited for it to clear. It took time in the still air. The sun had already burned off the previous day's rain. At last it settled, filming his bright paintwork. He winced and reached for a cigarette, lighting it with a snap and flicking the match out on to the ground where it could do no harm, there not being a single blade of grass it could catch light to. He got out, wearily, not knowing quite where he would begin. He guessed they would know it was about the lynching, but would they know about what seemed to have followed? Was it them that did it, whatever it turned out to be?

Even if it was not, he felt sure they would know and equally sure that they wouldn't say a thing. Not saying a thing to the law was the one lesson they learned and that before they were sent off to school, in case they encountered the law there and let on before they had been taught all the rules of the tribe. He waited to see if anyone would appear. They did not, so he made his way up on to what must once have been a porch but had evidently decided to slide down into the ground, one end tilting toward him. He climbed the steps, splintering beneath him. The outer door was open. What once had been a screen was now no more than a rusty mesh, torn and holed like the stockings of some old woman down on her luck.

'How you do'en?' he said to the man who came to the door, a man whose age he could never have guessed to the nearest twenty.

'What you'm want?'

'Boys around?'

'What boys?'

'Oldest.'

'What you'm want them for?'

'Ask some questions?'

'They don't know nothing.'

'About what?'

'Nothing.'

'Nothing? Know their names?'

'What you'm want?'

It was as though he were stuck in a whirlpool. The man's eyes seemed blank, just staring at him, waiting for the next question not to answer. Something was wrong, though what it was he couldn't say.

'There's been some trouble.'

'None of mine.'

'Trouble the other night. Now trouble again.' Then something hit him. The dogs. The last time he had come, carrying a summons, the others having been torn up as he supposed, there had been dogs everywhere.

'Where're the dogs?'

'You want dogs?'

'No, I don't want dogs. Where are they?'

'Out.'

'Where?'

'With the boys.'

'Where are they?'

'Out.'

The day stretched ahead of him and he could see how he might be spending most of it like this.

'When will they be back?'

'The dogs?'

'The boys.'

'Can't say.'

'You had any trouble here?'

'What kind of trouble?'

'Anyone get hurt?'

'No trouble.'

'Why d'you ask what kind?'

'What?'

'Come in?'

'What?'

'Can I come in?'

The old man edged across to block the door.

'What you want to come in fer?'

'It's hot out here.'

'Don't run no café. Come back when it cooler.' Then, as an afterthought, 'Or don't come back at all.' He grinned, baring his broken teeth.

Then the sheriff heard a sound from inside, a whimpering, like a dog that has been whipped.

'What's that?'

'What?'

'That noise.'

'The wife.'

'The wife?'

'What I said.'

'Why she crying?'

'Damn knows. Why do women do anything?'

The sheriff did what he knew he would have to do. He stepped toward the man and pushed him aside with his arm.

'Here. Where you'm going? This my place. You get on out.'

He stepped into the hallway. There were no boards, just compacted earth, hard and cracked. He heard the sound again and moved toward it.

'You get out of here. I'll call the boys.'

'I thought they were out,' he said back over his shoulder.

'I got more'n them,' he said, but not that many, the sheriff realized as he stepped through a doorway into another room. Not as many as he had had, because there, on a trestle table, were the bodies of two of them and beside them an old woman, looking as like the man as you can while being a different sex, crying into a handkerchief that was mostly black and somewhat other colours as well.

'So,' said the sheriff. 'Who killed them?'

'Don't you worry about them. We get them for sure. Ain't nobody goin a do this and live. No, sir, that they ain't. Quit bawling. Ain't nothing to be done except kill they bastards.'

'More than one of them, then.'

'I ain't talking to you. You no business here. This my home and they my boys, now get yourself out or I'll get you out myself.'

'There's a crime been committed here and I'm not moving till I find out what happened.'

'What happened is that some bastard killed my boys and now they getting killed. They getting hunted down and they getting killed and ain't none of your business neither. Now get.'

The sheriff turned around and stepped out into the sun. Everything was as before. After a moment the old man reappeared, holding a rifle.

'Git,' he said.

'I'm gonna say you never did that, since you've suffered bereavement, but if you don't put that down, you're going to jail.'

'If you don't git off my land, you're going to hell.'

The sheriff stepped aside so that the sun was behind him and, as the man raised a hand to shade his eyes, took hold of the rifle and twisted it away from him.

'Sit yourself down, old man,' he said, indicating a cane chair whose cane was unwrapping itself so that it looked as if it were tied to the porch. 'Sit down.'

The man did so at last, and stared ahead of himself as though there were no one there, no one he was prepared to acknowledge at least.

'How did it happen? You'll have to tell me and if you won't tell me here, then you can tell me somewhere else.'

There was a pause, so long that he wasn't sure whether the man was listening at all. Then at last he began to talk.

'Told 'em not to go. It were enough what they did. What they did were right but it were enough. Leastways it's a fool that goes in the day when anybody could be waiting. More'n one of them, you see. Waiting for them, no doubt. Nigger lover and others. Jumped them. Shot them down. Don't worry none, don't need no law to settle this. They were ourn and we deal with ourn. The boys'll be back, you see, and then it'll all be over.'

'I'll need the bodies.'

The man stood up, looking up at him, hatred in his eyes. 'You touch they two and you'll touch nothing else. They'll be buried regular. They be buried in the church when them others is dead. Until then, they won't rest.'

'It's hot, man, and besides, it's a murder case. I got to get a doctor look at them.'

'A doctor. What kind of fool you? They dead. Ain't no doctor going a bring they back.'

'Not to bring them back. They've got to be looked at. For the trial.'

'The trial?' said the old man with incredulity. 'There ain't going a be no trial. What for should we need such? You git. You ain't needed here and you ain't wanted neither.'

The two men stared at each other across more than a few feet of dust and might have stood there for centuries without understanding how the other could inhabit this world. But the stand-off was interrupted by the baying of dogs. Both looked across toward the woods and three hounds bounded out, heads down, not searching for a scent now but heading straight back.

Behind them, a group of men emerged, seeing him right away since one of them pointed at him and then at his car. He stood and waited for them, scanning their faces, faces that looked much the same. There was something wrong, though it was difficult to put your finger on it. Some disproportion. Some distortion. They each carried a gun and one of them carried two. They trailed them or held them on their shoulders.

'Get 'em, boys?' asked the old man when once they were near.

'What he doing here?' said the one with two guns.

'He seen 'em,' he replied, not saying who that might be, but referring, as was obvious to all, to the bodies lying behind him in the house, stretched out on the trestle table, having lived their lives and laid themselves down for eternity.

'So?'

'What happened?'

'What's that you say?'

'What happened? What happened back there that brought them to this and what happened where you've just been?'

'They got theirselves shot.'

'Who did it?'

'That's right, sheriff, that's the question right enough. Who could of done it?'

'If you want to be smart, you can be smart in jail.'

'What have I done? Seems to me it's somebody else you should be looking for.'

'Who killed your brothers?'

'A nigger lover. Leroy winged him, though,' blurted one of the others, spitting a gob of black juice into the dust.

'You shut up,' said his brother.

'What "nigger lover"?' He used the words as if they were a piece of rotten meat he'd found and wanted to pick up with a stick. These people lived in another century, as it seemed to him. But, then, he'd been away from the state long enough to breathe some different air. Should never have come back, neither, wouldn't have done but for a wife that couldn't settle elsewhere and then chose to take off when he did come back.

'We don't know nothing.'

'I can believe that, only I can't believe you don't know who did this. What "nigger lover"? The same one you come near to killing? That one? And what have you done to him now?'

'Listen up, sheriff. This is family business. You ain't from here.'

'I've been away but I've come back.'

'You ain't from round here.'

'Tennessee.'

'Hell, this ain't Tennessee. What do I know about Tennessee? You ain't from round here or you'd know. They our kin and we gonna fix it.'

'Besides, they jumped the train.'

The oldest brother, and he knew none of their names and wouldn't have been able to keep them straight if he had, stepped up to the one who spoke and put his face right in the face of the other.

'I told you to shut it.'

You could see the spittle hit his face. He gave a jerk to his neck as though readjusting his head, and then pursed his lips.

So, they had got away and the 'they' meant there were two of them and that meant he could see how the crime had happened.

'One of them black?' he asked.

There was no reply.

'Time you was going, ain't it? Got things to do, I reckon. An' so have we.'

It was time to be going, all right. There was nothing more to be done here, not for the moment at least. And if they were on the train, he had to get it stopped.

'How long ago was this?'

They stood staring at him with blank faces. Then one of them said, 'I'm gonna get cleaned up, Pa,' and spun on his heel.

The sheriff went back to his car, filmed now with dust so that he could trail his finger along it and see a shiny black line as he had on the piano. He looked around again, not seeing how any family could have been raised in this place but understanding how, if they had been, they would have been as strange as these. These people never looked beyond themselves for anything. They were one animal, growing on its own, dying on its own.

The car started instantly. He liked that. His last he had had to coax as if it were a woman he wanted to persuade to a dance, not that he'd done that in a while, not in a long while. He spun the wheel. The men watched. The dogs watched. Nothing seemed to move, except him. Then he was in the shade of the woods, lurching from side to side in the hard-baked ruts that shook him around as though he were somebody's child that had been caught in the mud, that had done something wrong and was being shaken by its father. And somehow he had the feeling that perhaps he had. Now they had given him enough to be going on, they would be back out of there and on their way. There was a race, except he was sure he was bound to win it. If they were on the train, the man and, he supposed, the boy, since it could hardly be a black man, at least none that he knew, then they could be a long way off. Assuming the boys had come straight back from seeing them jump the train, that would mean two, three hours. It would take him fifteen minutes to get back into town and maybe a half-hour on the telephone. That was a long way for a train to travel, except that no train he had ever seen pass through had been in that much of a hurry, certainly not the freight. And this must be a freight because there was no way they could jump a passenger train. None the less, three or four hours could be a hundred miles.

It took him more than half an hour to get it stopped, but the news that came back when he did surprised him more than he would admit. Those he was searching for weren't aboard, but somebody else was. They found a dead body. They found someone who'd been knifed and had his eye cut out and that took him way beyond anything he had been thinking. You get a picture, he said to himself, even as he was getting into his car to start on after the train, and everything seems in place and then something goes wrong and you can't hold the pieces together any more. Like two jigsaws mixed in the same box.

He swung away from the office, wheels spinning, dust rising up like a sign from God. The problem was now, he said to himself, where the hell did they get off? And within a few minutes, even as he wound the windows right down to get a breeze moving through, his mind was getting to work again. He had been given four places the train had stopped: two stations, a watering place and one where a deer ran right at the engine as if it had had enough of life. Later, they found it in the cab where the engineer had put it for later. But that was later, when nobody cared much what an engineer might have done. The question was, which place would they have chosen to get off? And he was sure they wouldn't have jumped, not if one of them was winged. And that meant that the man they had busted up and burnt a little, as he'd heard it, had now maybe got a bullet in him and wouldn't be about to jump, not if he wanted to live. But what foxed him was the dead man. That didn't fit at all. Well, time enough for that when he got to see him, but meanwhile he was going to stop off along the line, see if he could pick up any trail, even though that meant pulling off the road from time to time. The railroad ran parallel but some way back at places. He wasn't sure he should have brought his Ford. He didn't want to go busting up the chassis or ripping out the differential.

~

As soon as the train had pulled away, they started climbing. It was clear to both of them that they were no longer going anywhere, in the sense of a place that had been in their minds, maybe, when they started out. They were getting away, putting distance between themselves and whoever might be following them. They were doing something that made no sense and that therefore might fool those who tried to figure what they would do. Climbing upwards seemed to take them literally above everything. It was true that the man could not shake off the pain, that his shoulder was worse than it had been, even if his chest was better, just smarting from the sweat but healing along with that. His hand, too, seemed better. The shoulder was bad, though, even if he would not stop and look at it, would not stop at all, driving on toward who knew what, like a bird will circle on a thermal, rise up when it makes no sense anyone can fathom since its food is far below, along with the water. It was as if up there it was free so that, even if it died on the wing, it would go on flying as it fluttered down, not finally being dead until it hit the ground, bounced and lay still. That way, it lived beyond its time, still flew even though the life had floated out of it.

Already the railroad was no more than two silver threads laid on the ground, while to the north they could have made out a smudge of smoke from the engine if they had chosen to look, as they did not, staring no more than a few feet in front of them, focusing on the rocks and bushes, watching out, perhaps, for a snake, though not admitting such, simply aware, as any from there would be, that there are things that do you harm. Well, what a thought. As if more harm could come to them than had, as if creatures that kept to themselves and slithered through the grass could ever do what men had taken it into their minds to do for no better reason than that they were men.

The day was ending. By climbing they seemed to still the fall of the sun, the land opening up ever further as they rose. Even so, at last its tip touched the far horizon and seemed to spread out, its colours bleeding along the lid of the sky. And now, at last, they stopped, stopped and turned to watch a shadow begin to creep toward them across the land, itself a hazy blue. It crept toward the lakes that sparkled, their brilliant blue mixed in with a shimmering silver. Neither one of them had ever seen such lakes, set down like a kind of grace among the brown and green, a promise for those in need of hope. The man said nothing, amazed at his own capacity for wonder. The boy, voice gone in the night, snuffed out like a candle, stared as if he had landed on another world, not knowing what to do except stare, letting it all spill into his soul so that he and the man could maybe know, now, why the birds rose up, drawing great circles in the sky, drifting high where they could see the blue and the silver, now being eclipsed by the moving shadow.

'Best stop here,' he said, looking across at the boy, who was no longer behind him as at the start, being younger and unwounded, except where the ache of his dislocated arm had made him stop once or twice and wonder at how the man kept on, being as wounded as he was.

They looked around for somewhere they could get some cover. It was still warm but it was fresher here, as if the night might bring something it never did lower down, so that it would no longer be like breathing warm milk. There was a freshness that made the man, at least, feel light-headed, though maybe it was the shoulder, too. He wanted to look at the shoulder.

There was a small dip in the rising land, a pocket handkerchief of close-cropped grass, as if goats or some other creature had been grazing it close. He pointed to it and they walked across, edging round a crop of rocks still warm from the sun whose tip was balanced on the purple line of the horizon so that they could make out the fretted edge of what had looked so smooth before. Then, even as they watched, it disappeared, for a second a single bright orange spot, like a minor sun, hanging there and then turning off as if someone had thrown a switch.

He got out his knife and cut a few branches. In all his years, he had never slept in the open, except on his own porch on the worst summer nights. He had never been far enough from home to need to do it, so he was unsure what to do. None the less, he cut the branches, figuring them as cover of some kind, trying to rest them on him as if they were blankets. But after trying this for a while, he pushed them aside.

Then he remembered his shoulder. There was still enough light to take a look, for the sky was a sheet of red where the hidden sun was spreading its light over the western sky. He eased the shirt off his shoulder and took a look. But the red light made it all look inflamed. He could see a darker area around the wound and saw that it had spread beyond where it had been before, but that was to be expected. Cut your finger and it was the same. Even so, it felt bad.

He reached into his pocket for the cream, but it had gone, dropped somewhere along the way. His fingers smelt, though, of the perfume. The cream had gone but the perfume remained and still carried him back where nothing but irony awaited him. He slipped the shirt back on again and lay back. After a moment, he raised himself and looked across at the boy, hugging his knees and staring out where the red sky was already shrinking into blackness.

'You OK?'

The boy nodded.

'We sure in a mess, boy. But at least we got away.' Then, a pause. 'I want to thank you, boy,' — another pause — 'James, or is it Jimmy?' — the boy said nothing — 'for what you done back there, for what you did in saving me back at my house and for doing it again at the river.' He paused, almost out of breath, certainly his heart beating hard, though he couldn't have said why that should be. 'Anyway,' he said, and then said no more, falling silent as a first point of light pierced the deepening black of the night. After a moment, the boy nodded, but the man saw nothing of this, lying back on the grass which felt more like moss and looking up as one silver eye after another opened on to the dark world down below. Then, an afterthought, 'And I'm sorry about your daddy. He shouldn't have gone in that door, but they shouldn't have done what they did.' Then, as though feeling the inadequacy of that, and protected by the darkness, 'He were a better man than they and if I didn't know that from what he did, I would have known it from what you did.' And that was that, a debt discharged in the only way it was likely he would be able to do it because, even feeling free as he did up there, already high above what had happened and those who were chasing after him, he still knew that they would catch him in the end. He had been born doomed. And if he had ever doubted that, then every now and then he was sent a reminder, as with his wife, as with his son who had looked on the world and seen it for what it was and decided against it, as he should have done if he had had the choice.

There was still warmth in the soil but the air was cooling already. In the morning, they would climb higher and then maybe down the other side. Maybe, he thought, they could cross the state line, a moment later realizing that it wouldn't make much difference, this whole land being the same. It was born into them, he thought, so why not into him? He was a freak of nature, leastways that was what they would think down here. And what do you do with freaks of nature except cut their throats? He had seen a two-headed calf once. The farmer thought to get him some money for it until a preacher had come and stood there until he cut its throat, saying it was a spawn of the devil and he should breed for purity, realizing, as he thought this on a Tennessee hillside with a black boy by his side, that this was a joke, that those who were after him had been breeding with themselves for centuries, as pure as you like, and didn't they have two heads in their way? Something was wrong with them, right enough. And what they did to me and to the boy's daddy, that was a sign of that. The devil's loose, right enough, he thought, and he's right here. Not the kind of thoughts to take into your dreams, but they were the thoughts he carried into his.

~

He had visited the first two places before the night came on, talked to those who manned the depots, if you could call them that. One served a lumber yard more than passengers, there not being many of those, especially with money hard to come by. The other was for coal and there hadn't been much of that and was still less now. They had seen nothing, of course, swearing they would have seen, were on the lookout indeed, since the company gave them instructions about those riding the rails. Not content with that, he had walked up and down the track, going far beyond the depot to the point where the train would have slowed, though he still didn't think they would have jumped, not the man anyway, though there was no knowing how bad he had been hit, not even if he had been, he supposed, since, as far as witnesses were concerned, the brothers came right at the end of the line. There was nothing there, though not knowing what it was he was looking for, that didn't tell him a lot.

The main thing against these places was that they were too close to where they would have got on, unless they had had the cunning to jump right off and double back. It wouldn't have taken much to fool the boys. Then he remembered the dogs. The dogs were brighter than any of those that owned them and he wouldn't have run the risk himself, if he had been running, and he tried now, as always, to put himself in the position of those he chased. So, being as scared as they doubtless were, they would have stayed on until they were sure they were free and clear. And yet surely they had had the sense to know that word would get through and so were off by the time the train was stopped. Now he was on his way to the third place, eighty miles some away, when the night came on and, though he went on driving and came to it, finally, no more than a water tower and a loading dock, there was no way he could do anything else. And there was no one there either, the last train having gone through. They had called through the timetable, vaguer about freights, which didn't seem to operate to a timetable, 'not as such', they had told him, and, according to that, it would be seven in the morning before one came through and not long before that when the agent came on duty.

He got out of the car, meaning to walk along the track, but

the last flare of red had thinned out and gone. He thought of driving on, turning some cop out to find him a bed, but he had had enough of people for a while and he had no more liking for the cops than he had for anyone else in the state where he was born but was damned if he would end up dying. So he went round to the trunk and got out the blanket he used to wrap his tools. Since the car was new, there was no oil on it. He had always kept his tools in a blanket. The old one he had tossed out. It kept the tools from clanging around, and he had simply transferred them as they were, dropping them in gas for an hour and cleaning them up so they would be suitable for a new car.

He went round to the front. The sky was already frosting with stars but he wouldn't need the blanket for yet awhile and even then not for warmth but only for comfort.

In the north, the nights had been silent. Here, the noise was deafening, with every kind of animal you could name calling out for another of its kind, mating in the dark. Well, none of that for him. He could call as loud as he liked and nothing would come running for him. As if to prove it, he stood by the car and cupped his hands round his mouth. 'Carrie!' he called, and then again, 'Carrie!' But he could have called all night and she would never come back from where she had gone, wherever that was.

Then he sat in the car and got to thinking again. Why the dead man on the train? Had he, maybe, threatened to turn them in? Had he attacked them? No weapon, though, had been found, neither the weapon he was killed with nor any he might have defended himself with or threatened with. Well, maybe they tossed it out where he would never find it, or took it with them, or maybe he had never had such. The man was a problem. The rest he thought he could see. The ruction in the store, the spasm of violence against a man who must have known his fate the moment he saw them coming toward him, the white man caught in the middle, the black boy not knowing where to run to and running altogether the wrong way, as if there were a right way, so that he ended up in the middle of something he didn't start but had no choice but to follow to its end. The man came out of another story.

He looked out of the window, where the sky was now white with stars, like the frost that used to rime his windows up north but which they never got to see down here, or hardly ever at least. And it came to him then. The man did come from another story. No telling how long he had been dead, not until they'd cut him open and found out for sure, or as sure as doctors are prepared to say. So, they jump on board, getting away from death, and there is death staring right back at them. But if that was the case, they would have jumped right back off again. He would have done. And what was the chance, after all, that there would be some killer on board? Well, there was a chance. The country was full not just of the poor but the crazy, too. And how did the poor and the crazy travel if not by freight? No one would give a ride to such as them.

He got out of the car and stamped his feet. If he was going to spend the night cramped up in a Ford, albeit a spanking new Ford, he would ease himself a bit. Indeed, he realized suddenly that he hadn't eased himself for some time and went off to the side of the road and pissed, adding his own noise and smell to all those already out there.

And having buttoned himself, he decided to walk down the line, though the only light was the stars and a sliver moon that flattened everything out. Even so, he decided to walk along. He walked on the ties, lengthening his steps, remembering doing this as a child, when each step was like that of a giant, so that you had to jump from one to the next. All he had to do now was loosen his walk a little. The lines shone on the top where the iron wheels had polished them over the years. He bent down and ran his hand along one of them, feeling it smooth, yet with small notches you couldn't see with the eye where a piece of grit, maybe, had scoured a small pit. He walked away from the water tower, figuring that of course the engine would stop there, putting the wagons further back. He figured, too, that whoever jumped aboard wouldn't have gone so close to the engine, with the risk of being seen. So, further back, a good deal further back.

He walked along the line now, balancing like a kid again, one foot flying out at times to stop him falling off, until he forgot what he was doing there and remembered his youth, not in detail, just the feel of it, his leg flying out and him telling himself he was a hundred feet up in the air like an aerialist, with a slip meaning sudden death.

Then he glimpsed something silver-white by the side of the track and stepped off to meet his death, plunging that hundred feet, except that all thoughts of that had flown away. He bent down and picked it up and before he realized what it was, he knew it was what he was looking for. It didn't matter what it was, though it seemed to be some kind of jar. What told him that he had found what he was after was the smell, the perfume. In an instant he was back in that house in the clearing, if you could call it a house. He was on his hands and knees in the dust and sliding out a shoebox that someone else had slid out only a short time before since you could see the marks and there was no dust where it had been pulled out. And he was smelling it and wondering what flower it was it reminded him of, except that that didn't matter any more because this was the place they had got off and he didn't have to drive on to the next and all he had to do was wait for first light, not even for the agent to come on duty but just early enough for him to see if he could pick up their tracks. This was where he could do with a dog, he realized. He envied those he lived among nothing but their dogs. But there was no provision for one in the budget he had been given, and besides, wasn't he supposed to work with his brains and file indexes and the telephone and not the kind of thing that anyone with no brains could achieve just so long as he had a decent dog?

He looked around, but the light was no good for tracking so he walked back to the car, not balancing on the line this time, nor treading from one tie to the next, but thinking, already, where he would have gone if it had been him that had jumped down from a train leaving a dead body and with no one but a nigger boy for company, assuming the dead body to have any connection with the two, as logic told him it ought to have, but knowing that if logic ruled the world, why did such things as music exist, or cigarettes, come to that? And the thought was enough to send him reaching for one, his match flaring in the dark, lighting his face, then dying as he drew the smoke down into his lungs. One thing was for sure. Away from here is where they would have gone.

He must have known he had been seen. Or did he? He had never asked that and wouldn't have been told if he had. Maybe this man did not know he had been seen, thought he had got away with it all and no one would guess. Even so, he could see that it made no difference. He still had the same problems. Indeed, if it were him, he would have been in despair as problem piled on problem, as though he were Job being tested by God who took pleasure in making each day worse than the last, each hour worse than the last. He looked up at the hillside, rising away from him, a black wall. One thing, he told himself, he wouldn't go that way, not burnt and shot as he was. Trouble enough without giving himself something else to tackle.

He was back at his car now, feeling light-headed at what he had found, at figuring out so much even if he couldn't figure out what was in front of him right now. Well, he had learned something through the years. Take a problem to bed and it was often solved by morning light. There was no bed here, but a brand new Ford would doubtless work the magic. He climbed in the passenger seat, away from the steering wheel, and bunched up the blanket to form a pillow. Before he let himself drift off to sleep, he lifted the jar to his nose and breathed in the smell of flowers. They stirred some memory of his own, but before it could carry him back, he was asleep, the jar on his lap, the animals calling to their own.

~

He wouldn't let us take the dogs, not even the one, and wouldn't tell us why. It were as if he had decided we should take them on without no help at all. We had just gassed the truck up when he told us. I tried to argue but you didn't argue with him. Didn't make no difference if you was family. Being family didn't save you from a kick in the jaw. And if that weren't enough, if not having the dogs weren't making things hard enough, Pa wouldn't let us go right away. Called us into the house where Ma was still putting up a noise, as if that could bring them back.

We'd just as soon be on our way, but he called us on over and said as how we wouldn't be going anywhere until we'd paid our respects. And what respects were these? They were dead. Thing was to get those that done it. That was respecting them. But Pa's word went, even if some on us had begun to feel that the time was maybe coming when it wouldn't.

We went inside, Pa snatching at our hats, staring at us as if he would just as soon it was us as them lying there. There'd been others had died, but most of them had gone in birthing, except the one got drowned, getting his foot stuck when the river were rising. This was different. We could all see that. Why else were we getting ready to take off and get them as done it? But right now we all had to go inside where Ma had set two candles at the head of the table. She had religion. Never went to church, seeing as she would get the back of his hand if she did, but she'd pray sometimes, just to rile him up as I thought. She had a picture pinned her side of the bed, a Jesus figure with a big red heart and a glow around him. He stood for that but nothing more. Now there was candles and she was muttering away.

I didn't know what to say and no more did the others. We just stood there and waited for Pa to say something, only he didn't. And then he were crying, sobbing away like I never seen him do before. And I could see that this had got through to him as I guess it had to me, except that nothing came except a choking feeling that I needed to get out of there and find them that did it and blow them away.

He stopped crying and held his arms out like the Christ in the picture.

'Boys,' he said, 'look on your brothers. They been done by Satan and his devils. One'n them black an' one'n them white, though don't make no difference which they be. They goin' to hell, boys, an' you going a send them there. And when you do that, I want for you to send them a message from me. Say that I damns their souls for eternity and may they burn for ever in his fires. But boys, before you send them to hell, I want you to remember what you seen here and let them know that you seen it. Don't send them gentle. Send them hard. Amen.'

I hadn't known how it were a prayer. Even Ma looked up as

if she had never thought to hear such a word come from him. And she waves her hand like she gone off her head, which I'm thinking maybe she had.

'Now get,' he said, and waved us away.

'You sure on the dogs?' I said, as we climbed up on the truck. There weren't no reply and, since it didn't make no difference what we thought as far I could see, I gunned the engine and we was off.

I weren't sure how we should go, except take the road alongside the railroad. They could've jumped anywhere, except I got him good in the chest and I didn't see them jumping out quick. And besides, they would be looking for the dogs and so wouldn't care to take to the woods again.

'What we looking for?' I asked, but no one seemed to know so I kept on going, thinking something would come up. I knew how the train had to stop sometime, to take on coal or water and such, and there were places where that was done, so I figured that was the thing to be doing, keep an eye open for them and drive on till we found them.

It were dark now. Wouldn't have been but for Pa calling us in, but for the sheriff who knew more 'an he should and would be off an' looking, I guessed. Well, it were for us to be getting there first. But what if they stayed on right up to the north? Then, I thought, maybe that was where the sheriff come in. He could call ahead and get it stopped. Then I thought, but if he did, he would get the two'n them and where would that leave us? They'd go off for trial and be burnt, but we wouldn't get to take 'em out. But they would know, them that was running, and would likely jump when they figured it safe. But how far would that be? I could out-think a buck when I was hunting, figure where it would go when it tired. They were smart enough, doubling back, using the streams, but men was different. Out-thinking them weren't the same at all.

I saw a sign for a lumber yard and pulled off to look where it was. We stopped and looked around some, using lights from the car. There were nothing to see and I couldn't figure what it was we were looking for. But it didn't seem likely. It was only ten miles from the bridge and if it had been me, I would have wanted to put more territory than this between me and them that was following. So we pulled on out and drove further up the road which weren't so easy with one of the lights out entirely now and the other flickering away as we went.

We came to another place where the train might have pulled in and now I realized how this was no way to find them. We'd brought the dogs, we'd have had a chance. Let them out to run up and down the lines. On our own, we didn't have no chance at all. We fanned out away from the line a way but couldn't find nothing. So we decided we'd keep on going, looking for God knows what. They'd hardly likely stand in the road and wave us down. And if they didn't, I couldn't see as how we would ever track them down.

Which shows what I know, because come about three in the morning, we swung off where a sign said was a water tower and there was the Ford, parked right up against the lines. It were his, right enough. How many new Fords you see around here? But had he found them, or was he just resting up? I cut the engine and we slowed to a stop.

'What now?' I said.

'What now? We take him out.'

'Take him out? He's the sheriff. How'd you know he got them?'

'Seems right,' was all Al said, though I couldn't see it myself.

'Then where are they?'

'He's waiting on them.'

He got right on out of the car and went on toward the Ford.

Then he comes back again.

'You comin' or ain't you?'

~

He had his hand on me. Just pressing down so I would wake. It was dark still, or a kind of silver-grey from the stars, though I could see where they were fading off toward the east. I was stiff when I woke and there was his face staring down at me. For a bit, I didn't know for sure where I was, but then remembered, remembered it all.

On the train, I watched him sitting in the doorway, the fields and such gliding by and the wagon rocking regular. His eyes was closed and I could see how all I would have to do was creep up on him and push him out. Then I would be on my own and I could jump out and make my way. I don't know how real the feeling was, but I know I had the thought, even put a hand down as though I were going to make my way toward him. But what would have been the point of that? He hadn't made me do nothing. It weren't him that got through his window and shot the two men, one of them dead, one not. I could have left him in the river. Fact was, I didn't, though why I couldn't say. Then again, I guess it were him that pulled me out the river and put my arm back in. Maybe we was better off together than we would have been apart.

It was cold and I couldn't see why he had chosen to wake me. There was nothing there but the two of us. I was hungry but we didn't have anything along. We had got some water on the climb. There were streams, all right, so we weren't going to be thirsty, but I could have done with some grits or something to fill me up.

'We'll get going first light.'

I wanted to ask him where. Where were we going that we had

to be on our way? There was no one behind us, far as we knew. They hadn't checked our wagon. Then I remembered what was in the wagon and realized that they would come looking for us for sure, excepting how would they know where he come on board? And besides, there was someone out there as had done it and maybe they would find him pretty soon and forget about us.

I could see how the sky was starting to lighten a little far off, but it was still too dark to see much above or below. I eased myself up a little and something sharp jabbed into my hand. It was a stone, sharp and pointed. I held it up, trying to see when the light wasn't strong enough yet to make things out.

'That there's an arrow,' he said, though I could see that clear enough myself now. I had seen arrowheads before. There were places you could pick them up. I hadn't expected to find one here, though.

I looked down where it had been and saw something else besides. There was earth around it and I had to rub it away before I could get my finger under it. It was a little man, made out of wood and little pinprick eyes with something fixed in them. He squatted down beside me and took it in his hand. A first finger of red shot out across the sky, scattering all the stars around it.

'I heard where Indians used to go up into mountains to die,' he said. 'Wanted to get close to the sky. Sometimes they took their children along with them. Or maybe I got it wrong. Seems to me I heard it some place.'

I wanted to ask why that would be, why anyone would go up to die.

'Closer to the sky,' he said, as though he could hear what I was thinking. 'See everything in the world, that's what I heard.'

A second finger reached out as if the red man were up there

and pointing the way. I put the arrow and doll both in my pocket.

'Not sure you should do that,' he said. 'Maybe they was buried there of a purpose. Sacrifice or something.'

Even so, I kept them in my pocket. I could see why they had come here, though. There was just this one place with grass like soft moss, as though it were set here so you could take a rest. Maybe that's how they saw dying back then. Maybe that's how it was. Except it wasn't for my daddy. It weren't for him at all.

I looked around. There was a mist on the mountain and it seemed to drift around as if it wasn't sure whether to clear. I could see how if we went up into that, we might lose ourselves, even if up was up wherever you were. Down below, it was colouring up as the red sky began to change into something else, a kind of thin blue. I could see the first of the lakes, though they reflected back the sun so that they looked like pools of blood.

'Ten minutes,' he said. 'Ten minutes and we'll make a start. The sun will burn it off soon enough.'

I wanted to ask him where we were going, but I couldn't speak and couldn't think how I should ask him. So I just felt where the arrow and the doll were in my pocket and got myself ready to be going. I couldn't figure why we were going up, but didn't make a difference as far as I could see. It were somewhere else and somewhere else was where I needed to be. The red fingers were pulling back now, as if they had lost their grip, and suddenly there was the sun, gold and bright and starting its climb up like we was doing. It had sunk down to the left, clipping the edge of the mountain as it did, and now it was rising up over on the other side.

~

How dumb could I be, he thought to himself, feeling the rope chaffing his wrist, always having figured himself to be pretty sharp. And now here he was being suckered more than somewhat. Who else would have parked himself right in the middle of the people he was chasing, he asked himself. There I am, just dreaming whatever, and an arm reaches in and takes me round the neck. Then a bag over the head and the door opened and my arms pinned back by someone with the strength of a gorilla. So there I am. Except that I know damn well who it is and it ain't no fleeing felons. Far worse than that. It's the boys with horseshit for brains, and though they were put on earth because there was nowhere else would have had them, they had managed to sneak up on me who was supposed to be so bright. One of them put his hand on my hand and pushed me back in, taking hold of my hands and running a rope around them.

He sat, tape over his eyes, hands tied to the steering wheel. And now, he thought, they would be after those others. And a fair bet they weren't thinking of a citizen's arrest. These boys had murder on their minds, if they had minds, and where was the sheriff, sworn to uphold the law, but sitting in his car and waiting to hear the shots? Worse than that, they had tied his hands to the steering column of his brand spanking new Ford car as though he were still in control.

He knew it was only a matter of time before the agent came along and let him go, but who knew how long that might be? No time to check his watch, just the hand round his neck and by the time he had a bag over his neck, all he had had time to see was that there was nothing to see. It was still dark, then, was all he could think. So, what, two, three, four? Not that they would be able to do anything until sun-up. Try climbing that mountain in the dark and they'd break their legs or even their necks. Well, no great tragedy in that, he thought, straining to hear. If it was the mountain they were thinking of climbing. Until that moment, he had been thinking of the fields behind him, but his first thought now had been the mountain, as if somewhere in his heart he had been clear about that all along, unlikely as it seemed, unlikely as it was. So where were they? Close by?

'Boys!' he shouted, assuming they were there still. 'This is a bad idea. You are committing a felony. Obstructing an officer in the pursuit of his duty. And if you do more than that, you'll get charged with murder. And don't think you'll get off with it either. They'll move the venue. Try you somewhere nobody knows you.'

'Won't nobody find us guilty of killing a nigger.'

He couldn't help himself. He couldn't have been standing more than half a dozen paces away, but the sheriff hadn't heard a thing. Well, he thought, I guess they are hunters and know a thing or two, dumb though they are.

'Just let me go and I can take them in.'

'They're here, then?'

So, they didn't know.

'No, not here, somewhere down the line. I was just resting up.'

'Liar. You found them, or you know where they are. They here, ain't they?'

'I don't know.'

'Save your breath, sheriff. First light, we out of here. Don't you worry none. Someone'll come by.'

'And what'll happen if you find them?'

'You know what'll happen.'

'Then I got to come for you.'

'You can try, sheriff. I wouldn't recommend it. Don't matter where you move it. You can slide it around all over the state, it'll come to the same thing. Besides, it'll be self-defence, ain't that right, boys? And there'll be plenty of witnesses, wouldn't you say?' He talked some more, putting his mouth close to the sheriff's ear, leaning in the window, breathing his words and the smell of onion, bourbon and decay. It was not an enlightening conversation, being terminated, finally, by an abrupt command. 'Now shut your mouth, sheriff. We got things to do.'

At that, the door swung open and he could hear someone winding the window up. Then the door slammed closed again and he could feel the pressure on his ears. They sure built them well, these Fords, he thought, in spite of himself.

~

The light reached the man and the boy before it did those at the foot of the mountain. As the previous evening had ended in celestial flame, flickering across the heavens, so the new day began with the same. Shepherd's warning.

They stood, side by side for a second, looking out across the surrounding countryside, seeing further than either had before, offered a vision that neither had been offered before they had come to this high place, driven there by events they could barely understand. Their lives had been separate. They shared nothing, not even a language, one having his tongue stilled, until God or some other force had taken them separately and shaken them together. They were on either side of a divide that had been opened up before either was born, and since history has not one face but many, it would be a surprise if they saw the world alike. Yet they had been brought to the same place and were in the same danger, depending on each other, not understanding but depending, and so together, as had no choice not to be unless one were to go down and the other up when going down made no more sense than climbing toward the sky.

It was almost silent here and the man realized suddenly what it had been that disturbed his fitful sleep. For there were no crickets here and no frogs, or if there were, no symphony of such. It was the quiet that had disturbed him and left his cool skin flinching in the night. A bird cried out suddenly, as if to contradict his thought, and he saw below him a grey shape begin to turn around in a circle, not rising yet, the land having given up its heat to the night, but ready, like them, to go higher than they had been before.

'Let's go,' he said, and they moved off toward the mist still hanging above them, a grey shroud closing off their view of what lay ahead. Earlier, it had taken colour from the sunrise so that it seemed to glow, like a line of fire. But now it was no more than a cloud, come down to cut off the earth from the sky.

It was more difficult climbing now. There was still grass, there were still bushes, but the rock cut through and it was wet from the streams that splashed and skittered down. They headed for the mist as if it were the concealment they sought, though both knew it would disappear with the sun. But they seemed so far removed, now, from what they fled that neither moved with urgency. After an hour, they stopped, the sun warm on their backs. The mist had indeed begun to clear above them as the sun warmed the rocks, but it was still there below, where they had passed through it, cold suddenly, wet, so that they seemed severed from the ground, floating free, except that there were other mountain tops behind and hills that breasted the mist, still glowing red, though now the sun was fully risen the sky had turned from grey to blue.

'Five, maybe six o'clock,' said the man aloud, though he said it to no one but himself. He was calculating when the train would have been searched but had no means of telling. The further off, the less they could know where they had dropped off. But how long could they survive up here? He had never asked himself this, simply heading on up because up seemed the best way to go. On the other hand, there was water, and after a day or two, well, who knew? They could maybe come down and make their way further north, jump another train perhaps. Except it would be better to keep away, not tread the same ground twice. Then there was the body. How had it come to be there and why was it as it was? Waiting there, as it seemed, for them to climb aboard, a curse waiting for them to be driven into its arms. Well, he believed in curses, as should he not who had seen more than one work itself out in his life? Wife, baby, dirt poor life. Who would have thought there was anything more, who would have thought he had only to enter a store and say that she got it wrong, the woman got it wrong when she called him what she did, to bring everything down on that man and then on him who only looked on? And not only him and the black man. Two more dead already and now the two of them waiting to see whether they would go free or not, the boy at the beginning of it all, already a killer because he had no choice but to be, and him who would never be free because of what had happened, because of what he had lost already that would never be returned.

A bird rose up beside them, hovering on the wind, catching the beginnings of the heat, staring at them as it passed, dark eyes, ruffled wings. He sat down, tired already and felt a pain shoot through his shoulder. He grit his teeth, so as not to cry out. It had come from nowhere, though he had been waiting for it. He unbuttoned the shirt with his good hand, thumb and finger inside, finger out, flicking the buttons open. He peeled back the shirt and looked down. It was inflamed and red with a blackness at the centre. There was a line etched around the red, marking where the poison had reached. The boy came across and knelt down, looking at it, as if there were anything he could do. The bullet had gone right through, so there was nothing to cut out. It was the dirt, no doubt, or maybe his fingers, from touching it. He pulled the shirt closed and smiled.

'It'll heal. The body cleans itself. There's things in there that fights all kinds of badness. It'll heal.'

The boy looked up at the man, hearing something that went against the words, but the man just smiled and buttoned up his shirt, looking where the land stood out clear now and you could see the sparkle of the distant lakes turned from blood to gold to shimmering silver.

'Rest a while,' he said. 'No cause to push on fast.' Indeed, he had begun to wonder whether they need go any higher at all. The higher they climbed, the further they would have to come down, and he was beginning to think of when they would come down, especially now he had seen his shoulder in the light and knew that there was another clock ticking that had nothing to do with those who might be chasing him. Indeed, he no longer worried over much about them, not being able to see how they would find the two of them, for how would they ever find out where they stepped off the train? No, it was his shoulder he was thinking of now, and then the food they would need before long. He was still thinking of the future, then, still believing you can walk away and not look back when everything he had learned should have told him otherwise.

~

It was because it was Sunday. Mrs Brandt always went to her daughter's on Sunday so they could go to the Reformed Baptist Church together. And since there was only the one car, she took her husband with her in the morning and dropped him off at the depot on the way. So it was that the agent arrived thirty minutes early and saw the Ford parked by the railroad line and a battered truck just back under the trees. It didn't make any sense to him and still less when he looked inside the car and saw a police officer with tape over his eyes and mouth and his hands tied to the steering wheel with a length of oily rope.

The sheriff rang two different towns before he got an answer at the third. Around here, it seemed, police worked nine to five, six days a week. On the Lord's Day, crime was expected to take a rest. He left it to them to organize men to join the search and then set about thinking where the missing couple might have gone. As to the boys, they could be anywhere. He doubted the Sabbath influenced them over much, and wherever they were, they had it in mind to shoot someone. Whether it was likely they would find what they were looking for was something else. The compass has four points and the fleeing pair could have taken any of them.

He figured the one way they would not have gone was back where they had come from, and even the boys would have been capable of working that one out for themselves. That left three directions. If they were going on in the direction of the train, you would think they would have stayed on board, except that there was the question of the dead man, which was maybe one reason they had jumped ship in the first place. But if they were scared, they would hardly want to walk in the direction of people who might be coming back to find them. That left two ways they might have gone. One was back the direction he'd come from the turn-off, cutting out toward the lakes. The other was up the hills or mountains, the hills being high enough to call them either.

The mountain didn't really seem likely. It was a good way to get yourself trapped. On the other hand, back behind him the land fell away and was open in parts so that they could be spotted more easily. If there'd been two of him, he would have split up, but there weren't and he didn't fancy waiting half an hour, or more likely longer, since the cop he'd spoken to had sounded half-asleep and not all that interested. He looked up at the mountain and back along the track. Then he remembered the jar he'd picked up and tracked along the line to where he thought he'd found it. At first, he could see nothing, but then he noticed where a stream dribbled down, brown-stained, from the hillside. Running his eyes back up it, he saw a footprint, or what might have been a footprint. More a smear, really. But a foot had made it. Well, maybe others came this way. It was a depot, after all. Then again, the boys would have gone one way or another and there were several of them judging by what he had heard. But since he had to go one way or the other himself, he decided to bet on the mountain. That was the thought he had had before and thinking it again made it seem more likely.

He left a note for the others when they arrived, telling where he'd gone and suggesting they try both directions. Then he cursed himself for not ordering up a dog which would have settled it for sure. It had been light an hour now. They had jumped the train maybe twelve hours before. How far can a young boy and a wounded man climb in that time? And where the hell did they think they were going? Which was maybe why they hadn't gone that way at all. He nearly turned around, looking up at where the mist stopped him seeing more than a few hundred feet. But what the hell? Right or wrong, the odds were the same. He walked across to the Ford and locked it, then got a pair of boots out of the trunk, boots and a pair of socks, and then locked the trunk as well. He checked his rifle and the spare rounds. Checked his side arm, that he had never fired except on the range. There were guns up ahead and if the boys had guessed right, and if he had guessed right, there was some shooting coming because there was no way he could persuade them to leave things alone. He walked along to where the stream came down, glistening now in the morning light, and stepped across the line and on to the grass, leaning forward into the hill as he scrambled up the loose shale, rifle in hand.

~

When we swung into the depot, there was a single light shining, high on a pole in a mess of bugs. They were burning theyselves to death. The Ford were off to the side but we saw it right off. Tying him up didn't seem so smart when once we had done it, but didn't seem much else to do, we want to get who we was after. Where was the two at? He must've known, or why was he here? So I says to Ralphy, we got to talk, find out what he know. He don't know nothing, he say, when I pulled the tape of 'n him.

'What you sitting here for, then?' I asks.

'That you, Leroy?' he says.

'Yeah, it Leroy.'

'You done a dumb thing, you know that. You think I'm going to forget this?'

'I don't give a fuck what you remember,' I says. 'Where are they two?'

'Could be anywhere. You know that. We're eighty miles or more from where they jumped. Could of stepped off anywhere.'

'You think that, what for you sitting out here in a fancy car?'

'You like it, do you?' he says, playing me for stupid.

'They killed my brothers.'

'Maybe,' he says.

'Ain't no maybe. They dead and them two done it.'

'Looks that way. A jury'll get to decide.'

'We already got us a jury,' I says. 'Where they at? They go up the hill,' I says, 'or you reckon they split cross-country?'

'Where's your dogs?'

Got it in one. Should of brought the dogs.

'Fuck the dogs,' I says.

'Probably,' he says. Then he says, 'Take this stuff off my eyes.'

'You be al' right you sit still. There's enough'n us to cover the points.'

'Think about it,' he says. 'Eighty miles and all they had to do was jump off on a curve. Could be anywhere. In a day they're out of the state. Leave it to us. We got cars and radios. We got … dogs.'

'They ain't here, you ain't here.'

'I'm just sleeping, or I was until you came by. Assault, that's what it is, you know, Leroy, assault. Can't look in the dark. Just catching some sleep, is all. Been checking the depots, seeing if anyone saw anything. Why would they get off here? I favour them just stepping off when it suited them. Untie me, Leroy, and I can maybe forget about it. Put it down to you being concerned over your brothers.'

'Concerned,' I says, 'that's what folks in the city feel maybe. Where I come from, we're fucking mad.'

'Go home. Take your brothers and go back. If we get on their track, we'll let you know. Right away.'

I looks up at the light with the bugs banging against it and I think of him parking in this place and I know they here. He's just waiting for light.

'They here,' I says.

'Ain't likely,' he says.

'One thing for sure, they not backtracking. They know we be following. You too, likely. And why they go on if they just climbed down off a train that would've taken them forward.

Only two ways they could go.'

There was a smell about the car. Smelt of flowers or something. He smelt like a girl.

'Leroy, leave it to me, leave it to us.'

'I reckon we just leave you. Good to be talking to you,' I said, and stuck the tape back on his mouth. I don't know that I was sure before, but now I was. They were here all right. No one would choose this for a place to sleep, at least not him. He got soft hands. He would have taken his smart car and driven to some place with a bed. No, he were just waiting for the light and now so were we. There were four on us and we could split up like we had back at the river. They were here. I could smell it as clear as I smelt the flowers on the man that called hisself a sheriff.

~

He was climbing now for no other reason than that he could think of nothing else to be doing. At first it had been to get away, put as much distance as he could between himself and the boy and that thing they had found in the wagon, abandoned and left to rot and be carried off where no one would know who did it. He had been running from whoever was following them, and he realized he had yet to see the face of any of them, being shot down out of nowhere, nearly died in the river, risen out of it and come to this place which he had come to think of as Indian land, though the only reason for that was because of an arrowhead and a doll and a memory, somewhere, of a story he had been told, though when and by whom was as lost to him as most of his life that was so much the same from day to day that there was no way to mark one off from another.

The arm was hurting him now. He told himself that it would

ease off, but he had seen the line where the poison was and had begun to think how it would slowly move over him until it stopped his heart. Still he went on, the boy behind him, silent, thinking on something he could never know since the boy couldn't talk, even scratching his name in the dust rather than speak it out loud.

Yet for all that, there was something made him feel settled, no, not settled, he thought, talking to himself inside his head, just at peace. He had travelled further than ever before, there being no reason before to travel except when he and his wife had planned where they might go, knowing they would never make it but imagining it all just the same. And he had never been so high. He knew there was land stretching every which way but had never seen it all of a piece like he did now, turning now and then to see the boy was still there, to see the earth stretching out brown and green with splashes of blue, flashing gold. Strange thoughts had started coming to him as he climbed higher. It seemed to him that he breathed less easily, took less air in, feeling light and faint even. He thought how it might be to be a bird, free to go anywhere, float on the air, dive down, fly off to somewhere where there was snow and ice. He thought how it would be to be free of the land that held him down, had always held him down, rooting him like some tree that had nothing to do but live and die and never leave the place the seed entered the ground. At last he stopped, tired, not having slept more than an hour as it seemed to him, though knowing that often he dreamed of sleeplessness. He did not look for soft grass this time, but settled in a rocky dip whose flat stones reflected the heat. He lay back on one of them, like a sacrifice laid out for the kill.

And how many days was it since he was home and thinking no more than that he would have to go to the store? Who would have thought so much could have been poured into that time, whatever it was, like rain filling a dry barrel and keeping on flowing so that you couldn't say just how much water there'd been. The boy sat at his feet, rooting in his pocket, taking out the arrow and doll and turning them in his hand. Then he started sobbing, the boy, shoulders heaving, strange noises coming out of him, not like crying but desperate. He wanted to reach out a hand to him, did, finally, sliding down the stone and reaching out an arm so that the boy just turned to him and buried his face in his chest, the chest that had pained him but didn't no more, that pain lost in another, sobbing as if all his life were pouring out. Who would have thought he'd be doing this? Taking a nigger in his arms. But that wasn't what was on his mind. What he was thinking was that here was the boy he was supposed to have but had died. That was what climbing so high had done to him, the air thinning out so that he thought strange thoughts. Here was how it might have been if God had not reached out his hand and stilled two lives, if it were God that did such things. Not flesh of his own but someone whose pain he understood, having suffered pain himself. And not the pain he felt now, even as the boy pressed back into his wounded chest and shoulder, bringing that pain back, reminding him that pain could switch around the body when it chose. The pain of losing someone you cared for, someone who made sense of it all as if there was a pattern, after all, a story you were living through. And what were children for except to keep that story going when you were gone, so that even dying had some sense about it? If you didn't have them, then this was all there was and this was not enough. You had to make sense of what you had, and there was nothing there to make sense of, as it seemed to him. Except, looking out over the land below, perhaps there was if you could only read what was written there.

But how to do that? Like a blind man, maybe, press your fingers down on it. Maybe the land was like that. And maybe it was only when you were pressed down into it you could read the message that it spoke, understand what it had all been about. After a bit, the boy stopped crying, but he didn't let go and they both drifted off to sleep, needing the sleep they hadn't had, needing to mend themselves by dreaming they were whole.

~

I lost the sense of it. Running off from the train was all we could do and we had to run somewhere. Going up seemed a place to go. I didn't have no other place. And there were something in the climbing after sitting in the wagon being taken somewhere you didn't know. And the white man seemed to have some place in mind. I looked in his eyes and could see he weren't going to give me up, though I killed a man. And after a bit, I felt calmer, seeing the railroad tracks far below and figuring they would never guess where we had gone. We had come aways and I didn't know where we were, no more than him, as I guessed. But being lost made me feel better in a way, because if we was lost, how could they find us?

And when I felt all calm inside, I got to looking around at what I could see. The world, it seemed to stretch for ever. My daddy brought me a book one time with pictures of the world and all the places in it. On the front was a picture of the whole world as if you could hold it in your hand, but inside he puts his finger on Tennessee and it just a tiny part of it all. He shows me the country we live in and though that big enough, it still just a part of it all. Now I got to look out over it and I could see that it were true enough. It goes on right to the edge and then over it for sure.

When we stopped the first time, I found the arrowhead and

the doll as if they had been laying there just for me to find them. I never seen an Indian, but they was here before we was. They gone now. The white man done them, too. But here I was, standing just where they had done and looking out where they had looked. And I didn't feel so scared.

And at night I got the same feeling, staring up at the stars. The whole sky was full of them, so that no one could ever count them. And they were further than you could reach. It got cold after a while and I couldn't sleep, and a whole jumble of thoughts came to me that I couldn't sort out one from the other, until I saw the sky start to lighten in the distance and the stars started to fade away like they had never been there at all.

His shoulder looked bad. He stopped and undid his shirt and I could see it were all red. He didn't say anything, but was quiet and serious. We climbed up higher then, until even he gave up on it and settled himself on a rock. And then it all came down on me. I weren't thinking of anything when all at once I wanted to die and I couldn't stop from crying and rocking myself. My daddy was gone. What they had done to him. I couldn't bear it. And him talking to me and me watching and doing nothing. And suddenly he puts his arm around me and I hold on and hold on, shaking my head as if I could stop it happening. And he held me tight and I could smell him but I was used to that smell by now and he were there and where could we go and would they catch us? After a bit, I stopped. It swept away like the cloud that cleared the sun just then and I looked out where you could see the lakes, far away and bright. And then I guess I drifted off to sleep, the sun warm on me, feeling safe for the first time, feeling how we might make it after all, him and me. And when I woke, I saw a light flash golden in the sky. For a second, I couldn't make it out. It was maybe God's eye, I thought, opening on the world. Then it was gone and I could see how it had been the sun on a plane that was now no more than a speck of black. And a while later I heard it, far off and distant, like a memory.

His arms were still around me but he was asleep hisself, lying there with his mouth open and a soft sound coming out of him. And I could see how he could just have left me, given me up to them, said it were me that done it and they would have believed him, him being white. That were the first time it came to me. He didn't have to do it and he had. I suppose it was because of what they did to him. Even so, he could maybe have bought himself out of that and wouldn't no one have believed me. He stirred and after a bit let go on me and I stood up. He didn't look so good to me, though I wasn't used to judging how a white man might look. I could see that his arm pained him. When he shifted a bit, his mouth pulled back and a frown came on his face. Then I heard the plane again and looked across to where I had seen it before, only it was closer this time, circling round like the birds did, using the air, maybe, to keep up.

'They're looking for us.'

I turned around as he sat up. He pulled the face again and half-reached his hand across his front, but stopped.

'I think, maybe, they're looking for us.' Then to himself, quiet, he says, 'How they know we're here?'

Then he says, 'We best get under cover a while.'

There wasn't much in the way of cover except for some bushes, so we wriggled under there. We could still see up through the leaves, but I guess whoever was up in the plane wouldn't see us. It got closer, though, the sun catching its wings when it turned. It didn't seem much up there. No more than the birds.

'It'll go after a bit,' he said. 'Don't worry. And maybe it's not for us.' I could hear in his voice that he didn't mean this or wasn't sure. 'It's maybe someone learning. Doing turns up there. Just the day for it.'

I think, maybe, he was saying it for me, but it went just the same. One moment it was up there and the next floating down in the distance, dropping down like it was looking for where it belonged.

'Just out on a practice,' he said, 'that's what it will be.'

We wriggled out from under the bushes and I could see him looking up above to see if there was somewhere better we could go. Then he says, 'There's a cave or something up there, where the water's falling. Reckon that might be a good place to be. Come on, James, Jimmy.' He remembered my name but had forgot what I'm called, but I could hear in his voice how he was trying to say he was a friend. He didn't need to do that. If he hadn't been a friend, we wouldn't have been here, up on this old mountain, watching a plane flashing gold the way it done.

~

He had to be two hours at least behind the brothers. But since none of them knew where they were going, that might mean nothing at all. He knew that he was maybe chasing nothing, that the two he was after were perhaps miles away in the other direction. The smeared footprint was doubtless left by one of the brothers following nothing more than his own inclination. And after he had been climbing for no more than a quarter of an hour, he saw the pointlessness of it. Why would anyone trying to get away climb up here, except, perhaps, to sit it out?

Nor was it easy to see where they might have gone. For the first part there was a path of sorts, where people went for walks. There was dog shit, the usual paper trail of sacks and Kleenex and newspapers. Higher up, there were rubbers, trodden into the mud as if people had just laid right on down where they were. Higher up, though, the paths diverged, trailing off in different directions before giving out altogether. Hill or mountain, this was big and there were a dozen ways they might have gone if they had gone at all. He began to realize that he should have waited, that there was no point in doing what he had done. And besides, maybe they had simply walked around and off the other side and were already five miles, ten miles away in just about any direction. He had got sucked up in this thing just like the family of morons. His job was to be cool, be a policeman. Instead, here he was on the side of some hill he had never seen before, chasing people who maybe weren't there and with a homicidal family wandering round with guns.

He shifted his own gun, fixing the strap so he could sling it over his shoulder. At first he had tried to climb with it in his hand. God knows why. Did he expect them to spring out on him? Well, two of them had already killed two people, three if the one on the train was their handiwork too, though he couldn't see how it could be. That was a mystery. They killed the other two, as it seemed to him, because if they hadn't, they would have been dead themselves. They? No, the white man. He was forgetting that one was a nigger kid. He'd got to thinking of them as desperados. Desperate, yes. Desperados, not likely, not likely at all.

After an hour, he stopped, breathing heavily. This was definitely not what he was used to at all. Already there was a view. In fact, off in the distance, no more than a mile, he guessed, he could see two figures. Neither one was a boy. If that was the brothers, they had taken their time. Then he saw a glint of light, a tracery of silver. Boggy, then, the run-off from the mountain turning it all to mud. So, not likely they had gone that way, though they wouldn't have known it, not at first. And if they had, would they have turned back? Suddenly the mountain seemed more likely, assuming he was right about the smell. All this because he thought he recognized a smell. Then again, even suppose he did, they probably made this stuff by the ton. Why hadn't that occurred to him before? Because it was in the middle of the night, because he had already despaired of finding anything, because he liked to think he was the great detective. Well, it occurred to him now. Or maybe it was theirs and just rolled off when the train stopped.

He took a deep breath. It seemed fresher here. He wiped his forehead with the back of his hand. Might as well go on up, he thought. At least he could see more from up there. But which way to go? Up was up, but this thing stretched out in all directions. It would help if they'd snagged a piece of cotton, dropped a cigarette pack, left him a note. Down below, he saw a boil of dust off to the north and another over to the east. Reinforcements. Soon, Tennessee's finest would be strung out over a mountainside looking for what was maybe fifty miles away. At least they'd be searching the trains, though, in case they had thought to step off one and on to another. Checking the roads, too. And what had they done, these two running away, running in fear and desperation? There would be those who thought they had done no more than purge the land of two people had no business being there in the first place, if you obeyed the Bible. There were lists of people you couldn't sleep with and that family had slept with just about all of them, even unto the tenth generation. It was maybe families like this one that kept everyone back from progressing wherever they were supposed to be progressing to. Half the crimes in the county were down to them, but people were scared because they knew they would be happy to blow anyone away who so much as mentioned them, having no more feeling than if they were stepping on a roach. Now they were up there somewhere with guns, feeling they were God's avenging angels.

He looked back out toward the two he had seen in the fields and worked out that there were maybe two or three of them on the mountain unless any of them had tracked off in some other direction. But where were their dogs? As he understood it, such as them never went anywhere without their dogs.

He started climbing again, pushing the rifle behind his back, glad that he had shucked his jacket, though it had been cool when he started out. He heard the call of a bird behind him and turned to see some kind of a hawk hovering in the still air, watching out for something to kill.

~

The other boys are bogged down. I can see them over there, hardly moving at all. Well, they got it wrong, that's all. And so did them others they went that way. Made tracking easy, moving hard. But I can't see them out there unless they hid in they trees out beyond. More likely they up ahead somewhere. Ain't got no gun, neither. I got that shotgun along with me. This were the gun that shot the boys; this the gun going to wish them goodbye. Can't see nothing, though. Too steep round here to get a view. Could have done with the four'n us. I said we should try this place first. Now just the two and plenty places they could go. They could maybe swing round the back, cut on down to the road again, except why would they do that, they don't know we coming? That the problem, though. They up there, they got a view on us. See us from way off. Cover here, but up thereaways I don't see none at all, excepting the rocks. Maybe there's cover in they rocks.

Travis tracked round to the west a way, keep a look-see that side. Can't tell how they'd go. Got a boy along, though. That slow him down, that and a bullet in him. I got him, no doubt about that. Only surprised me he got out of the river. But he took a bullet and got it in him still, I bet. This is better than hunting squirrel.

~

The cave was dry, but it had a curtain of water falling softly outside it so that they had to edge their way in. It smelt musty and dank and he looked around for the bats but could see nothing where it disappeared around an outcrop of rock. Though the water seemed crystal clear, a lens through which he could see the blue of the sky shimmering like a mirage, it gave the light a green tint so that the cave could have been at the bottom of an ocean. It was cooler in here, the water and the green-washed rock protecting from the glare of the sun. It was a place to rest, a place to hide.

The floor was sandy, except where it was seared by fire. They were not the first, then, to seek it out, and if he had thought it an ancient place there were Coke bottles to prove it otherwise, that and several rubbers like snake foetuses, shrivelled and stiff.

None the less, this was the kind of place he had been looking for, not knowing that he was, but pressing on, sure that he had a reason for doing so. And now here it was, cool, secluded, away from the eyes of circling planes. Not that he thought they were really for them, out there in the still air, flashing some message in the sun.

'This is the place,' he said, sitting down on the sand, his back to a brown rock.

The boy looked at him, surprised, thinking, maybe, that there had been a point to the climb, that he had known at the start where he was going and had found it now. He put his hand into the falling water, the ice cold seeming to slice through him, his hand disappearing and yet just visible on the other side, a shadow, not black, somehow, but a kind of silver. He pulled it back and it was shining black, though the green light made it seem something else, something he could not describe.

'Indian land,' said the man, waving his arm in a half-circle.

The boy looked at the Coke bottles and the condoms.

'Not that stuff. This would be where they would come.' He spoke not from knowledge but from feeling. It was partly the light, partly the smell, partly the feeling of a destination, of a place he and others had headed for.

He felt tired suddenly, and not from the climb. He had found a rhythm, swung his legs and even his bad arm so that it no longer seemed the struggle it had when they were lower down. The railroad lines below had looked like fishing line, so fine, he could hardly see them at all. He felt tired, as if arriving at this place meant he could give in a little, let it go.

Then the boy threw another fit. He had gone round the corner to have a piss, as he supposed, and now there came this noise. And sure enough, there he was, spinning round in a circle, his heels digging down and turning him about a centre. He knelt beside him, unlooping his belt as he did so, pressing it between his teeth, holding him firm with his one good arm. It was like landing a pike. All that life thrashing around, all that energy going for nothing more than the shakes. He thought that maybe he would cry out, unlock his silence, bring language winging back from wherever it had gone, always supposing it had been there before.

Then he was limp and sweating. Even in the dim light, he saw his eyes open and something come swimming back into them, some life, some meaning. The boy shook his head and the man released his grasp, took back the saliva-streaked belt, teeth marks cut neatly into it, maybe a smear of blood. Impossible to tell there, at the bottom of the sea.

Then he felt a sharp pain in his knee. He had knelt on a stone, thrown up by the boy's thrashing feet, or so he thought, but when he picked it up and went back to the cave mouth, he saw that it was another arrowhead. He held it against the silver fall of water and turned it slowly, seeing where it had been fashioned, shaped for the kill. They must have been arrow rich, he thought, to toss them away as they did. And then he realized that he had been right. This was Indian land and they trespassers, except that Indians didn't go in for curses as he remembered it, didn't even feel you could own the land. It was everybody's, just like the air, just like the sea he had never seen. And that was why it was taken from them, because they didn't understand the need for ownership.

He sat down again and after a while the boy came to join him. He handed him the arrow.

'Came from back there. You turned it up when you were fitting. Now you got two.'

The boy placed the arrowhead in his hand and then reached into his pocket for the other one. Side by side, they seemed different. The man leaned across.

'Different tribes maybe. I don't know nothing about Indians, except that they're dead. Most of them. This the place they came to die,' he said, forgetting that he had told him this before, or, if remembering, figuring that if you have only a little knowledge it is best to use it as often as you can.

The shoulder began to pain him again and he had an idea. He stood up and removed his shirt, unbuttoning it slowly. Then he walked across to the falling water and thrust his whole shoulder in as he had seen the boy put his arm in before. The cold was a shock but he kept it there.

'Water's clean,' he said, as much to himself as to the boy, who was lying back, tired, as it seemed, from what had happened to him. He kept it in the water for a full minute more and then stepped back, holding his arm out. The pain had gone. All feeling had gone. He looked at it again, but in the green light could see no more than a darkness the size of a fist reaching down to where his collarbone stood out. It seemed better to him. 'The body heals itself,' he said, nodding, as if agreeing with himself.

Then he sat down beside the boy and closed his eyes. His head sank back against the sandstone, shaped like a pillow, and he drifted away, as he had so many times in these last days, drifted away into some other place without knowing where it was, except safety.

~

Meanwhile, two hundred feet below, one brother signalled to another, pointing up where he could see a curtain of water falling from the mountainside, catching the light so that it looked like a sheet of silver. He had seen something in it, like a white fish swimming up, a fish waving around and then suddenly withdrawn. He watched to see it reappear but there was nothing to be seen except the falling water and he stared at it, trying to figure out what he had seen. He couldn't put it together with who they were after, but there was something strange and hunting has always been a matter of watching for signs, not the signs you expect always, simply signs.

~

Three hundred feet below was another figure. This one shaded his eyes and looked up. He could not see the waterfall or the cave, though water did flow close to him, discoloured, like tobacco juice. But he saw a movement ahead of him, ahead and above. It was one of the brothers. Couldn't be any other on this mountainside. He felt for his rifle, not to swing it round, not to ease a bullet into the breach, but just to reassure himself it was there. From behind him there was the buzz of a plane. He turned around and looked to see if it was close enough to wave, but it was out over the valley, looking where there was nothing to see, except the other brothers, stuck, as it had seemed to him, in the middle of a bog. He turned back to the hill. The figure had disappeared.

We missed them, he thought. Can't see them coming this far. The higher they went, the fewer options they'd got. Simple matter of geometry. Back there, it would have taken a hundred men maybe, spread out wide, to have had a chance of spotting them. Up here, maybe twenty would do it. He was half-tempted to turn around, wait them out at the bottom, try going back along the tracks. Why wouldn't they have gone that way, after all? Go back aways and then cut across in another direction. He had forgotten why he had been so certain they would have chosen to go up. But he couldn't turn around. Not with the boys up there. First, he had a thing or two to settle with them. Second, if he had been right after all, he had to catch them before they blew the man and the boy away. He kicked his boot into the hillside to get a grip and set himself to catch up with the figure he had seen.

~

They appeared through the curtain of water like beings from another planet. One second, they were silver shadows on the other side and then they were stepping through, not edging round like the man and the boy had done, but walking through as if it were a store-front window they had been dared to run themselves against. They stood there for a second, uncertain in the light, staring ahead, trying to pick out who or what was there. The water dripped off them, their clothes dark and sleek. Maybe if the man and the boy had taken themselves further in, where the smell of bats was stronger and the light poorer, they might have escaped after all. Or maybe not. These were hunters and not likely to give up when once they had set themselves to follow. It took no more than a second or two for them to see the two of them, slumped together, dead already, as it seemed at first, but only asleep as it turned out. And, seeing them, it took no more than a second for two rifles to swing horizontal to the ground and for one of them to make a sound in his throat that was more animal than human, a sound of triumph.

'Well, look here,' he said, the water dripping off him as if he were dissolving, melting with pure hate. 'A nigger lover and his boy.'

The man and the boy were awake and looking up at these two figures against the liquid glass of the waterfall, dark against the light background so that they could make out nothing of their features, but hearing the voice, sharp-edged, and seeing and hearing the rifles as they were readied. He was shouting above the sound of the water washing down outside and running, stained rust-red where it took up the soil with its trace of iron, down the hillside toward a man struggling in the heat of the day, upwards and toward where he had seen two figures dissolve in a cascade of silver.

'We got you 'bout right, I'd say. Had you down for what you was.' He took half a step forward, still dark to those on the sandy floor, backs pressed against the rock, tensed for what was to come, not knowing how but knowing what. 'Nothing to say?'

'I,' began the man, not knowing what he could say that would deflect the fate confronting him, recognizing, as he did, the two figures dripping water black as ink against the bright of the cave entrance.

'Shut the fuck up. We ain't interested what you got to say. You thought you so smart jumping that train. Well, we a whole lot smarter. An' you got a slug in you somewhere already, ain't you. It were me put it there, an' it's me that's gonna put some more. You, boy, who the fuck are you?'

He tried again to speak, to summon back the voice he had lost. Nothing came but a strangled sound, somewhere at the back of his throat.

'I said, who the fuck are you? You Johnson's boy?'

'He can't speak.'

'Can't speak? Dumb, is he, dumb like the rest of them?' He took half a pace forward, shifting sideways to let the green-white light fall on the face of the two he was after, moving so that his shadow no longer fell across them.

'See your daddy die? Should've been there, kid. We strung him high. Should've been there. Now we get you.'

The man looked around, knowing there was no place to go but looking just the same, as if the wall might open up and they could run, except he knew that they couldn't, knew that his body was past it anyway.

'An' you, nigger lover. Running off with a nigger. You like nigger boys? You a faggot? Got a taste for it, have we?'

He was working himself to what he was going to do. If they had stayed in the open, instead of burrowing down in here like some animal, they would maybe have had a chance. He smelt the bats, felt the pressure of the falling water, felt the sound itself. All his senses had come alive when he himself was going to die.

'You killed my brothers. Shot 'em down.' He stopped and a choking sound came from him, a sound that was a shock to the man, who had thought that whatever faced him had no feelings of his own. He stopped the sobs by crashing his fist into the rock wall so that a silt of sand filtered down.

The rising sun sent a sudden beam of light slanting up through the water on to the ceiling of the cave, splaying a rainbow across it. Both brothers swung around as if it were something more than the sun and, as they did so, the rainbow washed across their faces until they turned back quickly, ready, no doubt, for the man and the boy to fight for their lives. But there was no fight there. They both sat still, staring up at the men whose faces had been plunged back into darkness.

'You,' he said, 'nigger lover.' He stepped forward and kicked the man's feet. 'You done the shooting, right. You the one done it. In the back, too. Crept up on 'em. Didn't give them no chance at all. Nigger lover. Where'd I get you? Where'd you get the slug?'

His hand began involuntarily to reach across his chest before he stopped it.

'There, is it?' he said, twisting his hands round so that the rifle butt was pointing forwards, smashing it into the shoulder so that a scream echoed round the cave and he rolled down on to the floor. There was a fluttering sound and the air was full of movement, an exploding whoosh, a sudden thunderclap and a stream of blackness flowing through the air and round the edge of the silver curtain, both sides, through the narrow gaps.

'The fuck?'

The boy made a sound in his throat, and even as he lay rolling in pain, a pain that swirled around, flowing out from his shoulder, even then, the man thought of the boy, thought that he would maybe have another fit, there in front of the killers, though how he could think this, sinking into the pain, was more than he could understand or could have explained.

'Fucken bats,' said the other brother, speaking for the first time, though he sounded the same, as though he were just another part of the one thing. 'Fucken bats. Get it over.'

They both turned back again. 'Sit up, nigger lover. Time's come.'

The man fought against the pain, seeing its irrelevance, readying himself for what was to come. He sat up slowly, staring up at the two figures who had stepped out of nowhere.

'I brung something with me. Look see.'

He shifted his rifle to the other hand and swung the shotgun off his shoulder. 'Recognize it? It yourn. Let it go when I plugged you. Didn't think no one would find it, still less bring it along, right, still less carry it this way. You don't know shit. We got things for you. We got things planned. That other time were easy. Should've shot you down then, had our fun, then shot you down. But for them car. Well, don't make no difference anyhow, 'ceptin' it does, don't it, because you shot my brothers. That make the difference. Nigger lovers is one thing. Killing my kin is another. This were how you killed my brothers, this gun, and this is how you going to get yours. Brought it along special. So's you could die with the gun you used. Only I take you a piece at a time. What you say? You like that? Let the nigger watch till it's his turn. What you say? Got nothing to say? Dumb like the nigger? Or maybe we light us a fire, have some more fun first. You like that? You like that the last time?'

'Get on with it,' said his brother.

'I take whatever fuckin' time I like,' he said, swinging round, the shotgun pointing at his brother now, as if he weren't particular who he took. Then he swung back, shifting the gun in his hand.

'You ready for it? Said yourn prayers? Won't do you no good.

You going direct to hell, after I shot you up some, arms, legs, belly. What you say?'

'Take 'em now.'

'Take 'em now, sure, take 'em now. My brother think I should take you now, like you'd put an animal down in pain. That the way he is. Ain't the way I am. Why you kill them? Think they was trash? Think we all trash? Why ain't you talking?'

'Take 'em. The sheriff.'

'I don't give a shit about no fuckin' sheriff.' Even so, it seemed as though he might have forgotten the man they had left below, and who would have been released long since and was coming, surely, as sure as anything else. He held out his hand toward his brother.

'The shells.'

'What shells?'

'The fuckin' shotgun shells.'

'I don't have no shells.'

'What? I tell you to bring shells.'

'I thought for the rifles.'

'Shells, shells!' He was screaming now. 'Not bullets. I got slugs. We both got 'em. Shells for the gun so we could give it to him with his own.'

'I ain't got no shells.'

'The fuck . . .'

'You didn't say nothing.'

'Shut the fuck up!' he screamed and threw the shotgun down in the sandy earth, kicking it so that it slid across and hit a rock.

'We got the rifles,' said his brother.

'I know we got the fuckin' rifles. I wanted the shotgun.' Then, to the man on the floor, and calming now, 'Well, don't make much difference to you, I say. You gettin' it just the same. You getting it like I said. Knees, elbows, belly.'

The boy made a sound, a strangled sound as if he were trying to be sick, force something up.

'What the fuck you ...'

But they waited and watched as the boy struggled with himself until a sound came out that was not a moan or a gasp or a cry but a word. 'Me.'

'The coon talks.'

'Shutup. What he say?'

The boy struggled again and the word came, clearer this time, as if he had shifted something out of the way. 'Me.'

'Me what?'

Again the boy struggled, getting half to his feet, and again a word came out like a constipated man producing a bullet-hard turd. 'Shot.'

'"Shot"? "Me shot"?'

And then again, the man, knowing now what he was going to say and wanting to stop him, but mesmerized by the effort that was producing the words, mesmerized that there should be words at all from one who had stayed dumb in the face of so much, unable to stop him, though he raised a hand to the boy that he should stop, go back to being dumb again, though he knew it would make no difference in the end.

'Them,' said the boy, sinking back again with the effort.

'"Me shot them"? You some Indian? Pigeon talk?' Then the meaning of the words got through to him and he shifted the rifle so that it slanted down, pointed in the middle of the black boy who was trying to save a white man when white men had killed his father, the same white men who were going to kill him now.

'Don't listen to the kid. You can hear he's crazy.'

'Crazy, yes. Sure. He's crazy. I can hear how he's crazy. Crazy to fess up. Thinks he's savin' his white daddy.'

'I shot them.'

'Sure. I can see how you would. Yes. It were the boy. Seen his own daddy go. Watched it all, didn't you, boy? How'd you get the gun, though? That ain't your gun. That his gun. No white man going to give a gun to a nigger, not to a nigger boy, not to a nigger at all, he ain't. Even so. I see it. I see it. He give you the gun and tell you to keep behind them. They never think to find a nigger there. If it had just been you, they'd have taken you. There had to be two 'n you. And it had to be the boy. They would have watched you, 'spected you. They never would have thought there might be a nigger there, 'n if they did, never thought him to have a gun.'

'Get on with it. They'll be here.'

'Right. They'll be here. That's right. Well, nigger, I guess you gets to go first. You the one that did it, you gets to go first.'

'No,' said the man, half-rising, only to meet the butt of the gun on his jaw, breaking it and sending him back into the rock.

'Outside, boy. You getting it out there like my brothers did. An' you, you just wait yer turn.'

He reached down and grabbed the boy by the neck, pulling him forwards. Then, like a sheriff backing out of a bar, he walked backwards through the water so that the two of them seemed to dissolve. The other one looked down at the man, helpless now, as it seemed, blood spilling from his mouth. Then he, too, walked through the wavering cascade and was gone.

In a panic now, knowing that there were seconds left, feeling the shakes coming on and with pain running through him deep and true, he fell forwards, reaching for the gun, reaching out his hand, with blood in his eyes as well as down his chin. It was no more than ten feet but it seemed a mile, with the pain shooting through him and a wave of blackness rolling over him. He closed his hand around it and pulled it toward him, unable to move further, pulling it in like a rope in the sea. Then he was fumbling in his jacket, where the hand cream had been and where a purple stone nestled in paper, and found the shells, the shells that had survived the river and everything else.

The pain made him shake, the urgency made him shake. He tried to focus his mind, control his hands. He broke open the gun, dropping one of the shells as he did so. He slid the other one in and then groped for the one he had dropped, not seeing, with the blood, feeling in the dirt and finding it at last, smeared with grit so that he had to take another few seconds wiping it on his jacket. Then he slid that in, hearing the pop as it went in. He snapped it closed and tried to stand. His head swam. Though there was a bright light now where the sun had cut through in a beam like a searchlight, he could feel a darkness begin to welcome him.

He banged his hand, the one holding the shotgun, against his shoulder so that his body lit up with pain. Then he took a step forwards as two shots rang out, sharp and clear, not a shot and an echo but two shots so crisp, separated by no more than a second, that he knew what had happened without needing to see. They had stood side by side and shot the boy together so they could both say they did it. They had shot the boy who had saved him not once but twice and no matter what happened now, there was no getting him back. And this was the boy that had told them what was only partly true, that had spoken for him as he hadn't spoken for himself. And he didn't think black and white, though that was why this had started. He thought how they had killed his son, knowing it wasn't his son but knowing no other word that could describe his feeling.

He stepped back now, knowing there was no point in going through the water, knowing that it was better to wait for them when they came back through, but knowing that it made no difference in the end whether he got them or they got him because what was important was what had already happened. For a second, he thought that maybe they had been shooting to scare and that he might still save him. But he knew that such as them, riled as they were, wouldn't see the point to that. Besides, those shots were as final as anything he had heard. It was an execution without benefit of judge or jury. It was the end of time.

He saw them on the other side of the water, saw their outlines, dark and wavering. And he saw their shadows cast on the back of the cave by the searching sun, as if some record of such as they would be imprinted for ever there. Then they stepped on through, silver for a moment, as though they had turned to molten glass, except that a second later they were dark and dripping water and with no faces he could see, the light coming from behind, so that he never saw their faces as he fired, not noticing which was which as they flew back through the water again, one, then the other, the second not moving, as if he couldn't understand what was happening, couldn't think what to do. They went back as if they were on their way to the planet they had come from, stepping into another time.

He stood with the gun in his hand, frozen, all pain suddenly swept away as though someone had been pressing a rock on him and had suddenly relented. Then the gun was on the floor quite as if he had meant to drop it there, except that he hadn't, was unaware it had gone. Then he was on the floor, too, sitting down with no recollection of meaning to.

After a minute or two, he edged himself backwards until he came up against the rock where he had been sitting before. He eased himself up against it and settled himself. There was no running any more. Just a blankness where everything had been. Just the sound of the water falling down. Minutes passed and he began to wonder whether he should step outside, see to the boy maybe. He didn't doubt he was dead, no more than he doubted the other two were, having taken buckshot from no more than six feet and straight in the chest. But he had seen enough of death and wanted to see no more, and since all death was of a piece, it reminded him of others and took him off to another time.

He reached in his pocket and found the package he had felt when he was reaching for the shells, the shells he had forgotten and they had known nothing of. He took it out and shifted himself along to where the sun had slid down the wall as it rose in the sky somewhere beyond the silver curtain of water. He slid along to where it shone warm on his face, bent and changed by the water, softened so that it was more green than gold. He opened the paper, which was no more than a newspaper with long-ago news, and there was the brooch and the purple stone at its heart. He held it up where the sun could reach it, watching as a light seemed to pulse at its very heart, as if it were alive and had been all these years, though the woman who'd worn it had been dead in her grave, her and the one she died in bringing into the world. And as the light flickered and moved, bending and twisting like a candle in a breeze, so he remembered what he had tried so hard to forget, tried to bury deep where he could never hope to reach it. And he sat there, staring at the stone, remembering not only her but what he had been before the world had pressed down so hard on him that he had forgotten what had once lifted him up so high. And somehow, along with that memory was another now, not a memory, perhaps, since it came to him from but a moment ago, but a face, a face staring up at him as if he might turn aside what must come. And if one was white and one was black, what was that to him? The stone he held in his hand had a colour, too. It was not the colour that mattered but the flame that flickered at its very heart.

He was scarcely aware of reaching into his pocket again, feeling the shells there, so reassuring to the touch. Scarcely aware, either, perhaps, of taking two out and laying them in his lap while he wrapped the stone up in its fading newspaper nest. He reached forward for the gun and broke it open, running his hand along the barrels before lifting it so that he could look along those barrels, pointing it at where the sun came through, where the blue of the sky spread out as though you looked at it through the thinnest gauze. Two perfect circles of light. Two circles of blue like eyes staring down at him. Then he closed it up and smiled to himself. He had come up high, higher than he had ever been before. Outside, he knew, the world stretched away in every direction. Things lived and died and it made no difference. There was no time and regret was no more than a drop of rain in spring. Living in a room, in a cabin, on the edge of a wood, with nowhere to go but the outhouse or to a town where people lived in themselves, he had never understood all of this. It was coming up high that had taught him, and how could he be sorry, then, to have come so far or to have risen up like the birds he knew were no more than fifty feet away, beyond the clear lens of the water, floating ever higher and seeing ever further? His lips began to move, lips cracked and flecked with blood, and though his broken jaw made it difficult to open his mouth, began to sing to himself a long-ago song. 'Beautiful dreamer,' he sang, and then again, 'Beautiful dreamer,' not remembering any other words, but hearing, even in this cave on the top of the world, where water fell like a silver shroud, the broken sounds of a broken piano which none the less brought forth beauty and harmony.

~

He heard the two shots, spaced by no more than a second and sharp. Rifle shots. Two shots, two people. These weren't signal shots. They were the sound of people dying.

'Fuck them,' he said aloud, 'fuck them, fuck them, fuck them.' And though he knew now that it could hardly make a difference, that he was too late, had delayed too long, even so scrambled forwards, tearing his hands on the rocks, slipping where the hillside was slick with water.

He was alert. Now it was murder, murder virtually before his eyes. And maybe those who could do what they had done would think nothing of taking him out. It wouldn't save them in the long run, but if he was dead, that wouldn't help him at all.

Then, two more shots, a shotgun this time. So, they had finished one with the rifle and the other with a shotgun. Maybe that was their style. They even shot black people with different guns. Nothing would surprise him about them.

He slowed down, taking it more carefully this time, pretty sure what he would find. Then, no more than five minutes after the first shots, there came another. The shotgun this time, though sounding odd, echoing hollow as if someone had fired it at the bottom of a mine shaft. And what was he to make of that? He had thought he had got it clear in his head. Two inbred killers hunting down their prey. But that couldn't be. Where did the shotgun fit in, a shotgun fired five minutes after he had thought it was all over? Was it the boys having their private fight? No sense at all. Not until he came to the cave, and then a sense of sorts began to appear. But not really. He still couldn't account for what he'd heard.

Down below, he could see other men climbing up toward him. Off to the side, a plane was banking in his direction. But in front of him was a dead black boy, his face gone, twenty feet from the waterfall, and, closer to the waterfall, the brothers, each blasted from up close and both wet through. There was no point in checking them. They had been dead the moment they were hit. That left the man and that left the final shot.

As he stood there, a sudden swirl of black swept past his head and he crouched instinctively, bringing his rifle up. But they were past him, the bats, returning to their cave, pointing the way meanwhile to a man who was feeling the world slip away from him.

He edged in, not stepping through the water but keeping his back to the green-slimed rocks. Despite the sun, filtered through the waterfall, he did not see the man at first, though he already knew that was where he must be. It was strange, being inside with the water falling down, the sound of the water setting up a constant note. Then he saw him, one sock off, shot in the chest. Not many went for the head. Didn't like to think of themselves going to eternity like that. Indians, he remembered reading once, thought that if your eyes were taken out, you couldn't see to find your way to eternity. There was nothing else to see. Just a dead person putting an end to a story he had tried to figure out, always too late to play a part in it. But that was the nature of his job. Other people wrote the story. Your job was to make sense of it.

It was a crime scene and by rights he should just have left

everything as it was, but he didn't like that bare foot. There was nothing dignified about almost any of the deaths he had seen, people pulled from lakes, all puffed up, faces wrong, pieces chopped off by machinery. But the bare foot bothered him, so that, without thinking really, he bent down and picked the sock up. He'd had to do it, of course, to get his toe on the triggers, both triggers, not just one. Even so, what did it matter if he slipped the sock back on? So he knelt down in front of the man and lifted up his foot, not looking higher than his waist, not thinking anything about what had killed him. But as he knelt, he felt a sudden pain shoot through his knee.

'Jesus,' he said, the sound echoing round a cave now washed with a flickering rainbow. He lifted his knee and slipped his hand down to shift the stone. Only it wasn't a stone. It was an arrowhead. He lifted it up to the light. He had seen plenty of these in his time. He could see where the stone edge had been chipped away to shape it. He shook his head, tossed it down, and then turned back to the foot resting on his thigh, and slid the sock on carefully, not knowing why he was doing it except that it looked wrong for him to be sitting there with one bare foot as though it were some kind of a joke.

When he had finished, he wiped his hands on his pants and looked down at the man, his face tilted back and the light flooding over it from red to violet. Then he bent down and picked up the arrowhead. He took it to where the stream was falling, a waft of cool air raised by the passing water. He ran his finger over the sharpened point and then, looking back at the man you could almost believe had fallen asleep if you didn't look at where he had blown his heart away, he shrugged, turned back to the shimmering crystal of the waterfall, and, for no reason he could have explained, drew back his arm and threw the arrowhead with all the force he could summon. It flew through the trembling sheet of water and disappeared into another time as if it had been fired from a bow and not thrown by a hand, as if then and now were the same. It rose, a shiver of gold against the sun, and then, as a distant bird turned slowly around an invisible centre, curved down toward the waiting land. It is falling yet, as in a dream without ending.